" . . . as the waste expands all around him, as the oxygen rushes in, Forrest is falling. Part of a great wad of garbage which tumbles down the steep slope, turning end over end . . . "

WASTEFALL

STEPHEN E. MILLER

PULP PRESS
Vancouver

Published by
PULP PRESS BOOK PUBLISHERS
100-1062 Homer Street
Vancouver, B.C. Canada V6B 2W9
A Division of Arsenal Pulp Press Book Publishers Ltd.

The Publisher gratefully acknowledges the financial assistance of the Canada Council.

COVER ART AND DESIGN: David Lester
PRINTING: Hignell Printing Ltd.
TYPESETTING: Vancouver Desktop Publishing Centre Ltd.
PRINTED AND BOUND IN CANADA

CANADIAN CATALOGUING IN PUBLICATION DATA:
Miller, Stephen E., 1947-
Wastefall

ISBN 0-88978-220-2

I. Title.
PS8576.I44W3 1990 C813'.54 C90-091132-8
PR9199.3.M54W3 1990

SILVER

Forrest grins, pleasantly drunk, with one elbow on the edge of the stage as the stripper dances above him. She is stunning and beautiful and perfect, with perfect oiled breasts beneath the cold blue light. There is glitter on her eyelids and on her skin. He sees immediately why they call her 'Silver'—for the hair is somehow made metallic, like finely spun aluminum foil, even her pubic hair—unusual and different!

Her eyes sweep through the room taking in the audience and then returning—always returning!—to Forrest.

He grins.

She glides, swirls, across the stage beneath the lights which are beginning to pulse in rhythm to the music which is inspired by the pulse of the city all around them. Electronic, flickering, machine-like.

As Silver dances she seems to be undergoing an emotional change. Forrest watches her closely, trying to figure it all out.

The dance is growing, it has a *theme!* When her dance becomes less mechanical, less robotic, her face becomes more expressive.

Forrest, now alert to this entertaining puzzle, examines her. Leaning back, with his heels leisurely hooked over the rung of the stool under him. Casual. He is analytical and aware. Poised and cool, and *settled* there beside her stage.

Then at the peak of one of her lithe movements, an arch, a stretch, she seems to suddenly gasp—

She is trying to keep from touching herself! He suddenly understands!

Forrest nods in realization as Silver presses her hands down between her legs. She touches her silver panties and her hand draws back sharply. As if she has encountered a stinging substance; a nettle, a bumblebee. But Silver is starting to smile and Forrest decides this pain is not too terribly uncomfortable for her.

Deftly, smoothly, she slides the panties away from her body.

What is so arresting is that she looks at him, right in the eye, when she does it.

"What about you?" comes a bass voice.

Looming in from Silver's direction, blocking Forrest's view, is a man's face. Forrest stares up blankly, not remembering the question.

"Forrest," he says giving his name to his teacher.

"Blue?" asks the man.

"Blue?" says Forrest.

The man puts a beer in his hands and goes away.

Forrest looks down and tries to focus on the beer glass in his hand.

Blue.

Right. He aims it toward his mouth, but spills a gush of it down his shirt front. Saving most of it, he gets a drink, sets the glass down and settles back.

The music reaches a frenzy as Silver finds a pole on her stage and begins pressing her groin against the metal.

It seems to Forrest that her emotions are beginning to get the best of her—the music peaks and she opens her eyes—*right at him!*

"Yeah!" comes a voice that Forrest realizes is his own.

Liberated from her machine persona, Silver begins spinning about the perimeter of the stage. When she comes by he inhales deeply and can smell her perfume.

" . . . Silver, Silver, Silver!" calls a woman's voice in appreciation over the speakers. There is a smattering of applause. Forrest begins slapping his palms together in acknowledgement.

She retrieves her minimalist clothing and casts one last look over her shoulder. Looking at him, wanting him!

"Silver!" says the woman's voice once more.

There is applause. Whistles.

"Goddamn . . . " Forrest mutters under his breath, enthralled at the pageant of it all.

"The fucksa matter!" comes a voice from somewhere behind him. Something seems to have suddenly bumped against the back of his stool.

Forrest turns and stares into the blurry angry face of a huge man. The main thing that Forrest can see is the man's nose, a thick nose with curly black hairs growing out of it.

"You like my girl?" says the man, pushing the horrible nose closer to Forrest. Forrest is aware that he has probably drunk too much tonight. A wave of nausea begins to wash over him.

"Wha—what?" Forrest blurts, trying to unhook his shoes.

The man puts a meaty hand on the shoulder of Forrest's jacket. He begins to rub the material between his thumb and forefinger, giving little tugs on the cloth to punctuate his speech.

"You-like-my-girl?" he says, spraying Forrest with his spit.

Forrest's mind begins to whirl. There's no sense here at all. Is Silver the—the *friend* of this hulk?

The huge man has scrunched up his eyes. He no longer is looking at Forrest, his head is hanging down, weaving from side to side with the beat of the music.

"Amber!" comes the enthusiastic voice of the announcer.

The man gives a terrific wheeze and raises his head. It is like a whale breaching. The thick black hair falls down over his forehead.

"You like her, don'cha?"

Forrest looks up and the girl has changed, it's not even the same girl anymore.

"Yes, but she's different now," he tries to explain to the ugly nose.

"*My* girl," the man says, firmly pounding his chest and

sitting straighter on the stool, "You don't like my girl." This last is a statement, not a question.

"No, I like her, sure I like her." The man gives a sharp little tug on Forrest's lapel.

"She's not different, I'm the one that's different," he says with gravity.

"No, I mean, she's not your girl, she's changed," he says with a shrug, trying to be friendly.

The man frowns.

Forrest points at the stage. "She's not your girl anymore," Forrest tries to explain, but obviously the huge man doesn't understand. He tries to stand, but falls against the edge of the stage, gets his balance and pushes the hairy nose closer to Forrest.

"Wanna bet?"

Forrest, beginning to panic with the dangerous absurdity of this conversation, turns to regard the newest girl who is nervously trying to distract them by turning away from them and touching the toes of her high heels. For a moment it almost works.

"You see," says Forrest helpfully, "she's changed, your girl has gone."

Forrest sees that the man, now that he is standing, is big. Really big, a heavyweight wrestler, a stevedore, someone who uproots trees for a living.

The gigantic head waggles from side to side. His gaze swivels from Forrest up to the stage for a moment. He rocks back and forth while he waits until he can see her face.

"Eeeeeehh . . . eeehhh . . . . "

Suddenly Forrest is aware that the huge man has begun to cry!

Great tears roll down the hairy cheeks, a long string of snot begins to ooze from the grotesque nose and Forrest feels the churning sensation in his stomach again. It's time to leave.

"Rachel!" screams the big man. The girl on stage leaps around nervously.

"Rachel! Goddamn it . . . ooooooohhhh." He begins to howl—a long swooping sound like a dog seeking its master.

Once again someone has started bashing into his chair. Other huge hands are grasping Forrest.

"He's looking for his girl," Forrest tries to explain, but suddenly there is a great earthquake and it is as if several of the equally large men who serve beer around the stage have decided to attack them both.

"Rachel!" howls the big man.

Now someone is pulling Forrest away from the stage. His beer glass falls and shatters on the floor. A stool goes flying, tripping him, but even before he can fall muscular hands are lifting him by the collar.

Forrest finds himself being efficiently moved by the competent hands down a grubby hallway behind the stage.

There is a mop, a pail. A storeroom, a toilet flushing.

"Ruby . . . Ruby . . . Ruby!" calls the distant woman's voice.

As he clatters down the narrow hall there is a slash of light from a curtain being pulled aside and a face comes out to stare at him.

Her eyes lock and then move from his, down to his soaking pants and back up again.

Silver . . . .

ON THE WATERFRONT

" . . . and don't come back again, sir."

Rising from the wet pavement of the alley, Forrest realizes that he never got a good look at his assailant. Just a pair of hands.

The rear door slams behind him, and he flinches at the sound.

His first steps only send him to his knees in a grimy puddle. He can't walk anymore! Did he break a leg, twist an ankle?

He crawls for what seems like miles, away from the huge hands, the woman's voice, the spangles, the glitter.

Eventually he gets tired and stops crawling, finds the friendly masonry of a wall and leans against it trying to figure the injustice of it all.

The alley extends deeper into the merchant district, past the service entrances of stores, the long blank side of a parking lot.

He hungers for a better section of town. Music, neon, people, anything except this grimy . . . *industrial* wasteland.

The alley goes on forever. It makes T-intersections with other alleys, leads him into streets he's never seen, dark and dangerous areas. He has the queasy feeling that animals are watching him from the shadows.

His progress becomes rhythmic. He crawls, falls, staggers; crawls, falls, staggers. Hides from a police cruiser when he sees one. Why he hides, he dosen't know, but anywhere is better than the drunk tank.

He finally stops to urinate, his forehead leaning against the cold brick of a factory wall, struggles to do up the pesky fly and looks for a place to stop for awhile.

It is getting chilly. He is tired, exhausted, dragging his feet along. Across the alley is a huge blue metal trash container, crates and boxes, and now the wind is coming up, raw and wet from the harbour.

What the hell. Forrest boosts himself up so that he can peer over the edge of the container. There seems to be a lot of cardboard and paper piled up in there, big mailing tubes, metal packing ties, department store shit.

Starting to rain.

Stay out in the rain, walk for miles and get pneumonia—is that an option? Does that make any sense?

Climbing into the container is difficult, a real Olympic-level challenge, but there is a chain link fence to wedge the toe of his shoe into; mercifully the steel lid is already propped open.

And now he is straddling the sharp edges, looking down inside the container below him, cardboard, beautiful cardboard. Swinging his leg over he falls into the tangle of packing, the metal strapping ringing against the sides of the container; a spray of shredded paper finds its way into his hands. He pulls it over his chest and slithers, burrows deeper into the container, pulling his knees up and jamming his hands down into his crotch.

Safe.

Above him the slash of the lid of the container, and a tracery of stars.

A constellation takes shape above him, turning slowly with the motion of the Earth. Long legs, arms that reach out toward the heart of the city, a head with one bright eye, hair that trails out until it is blocked off by the buildings above him.

She turns, she spins, she dances.

Spangles and glitter, he thinks. Forrest heaves a great sigh within his warm bed of packaging materials. The metal strappings twang in response. He smiles as he watches the star-woman above him.

In the distance he can hear the howling of the man with

the huge nose. The sound soars and rebounds in the canyons of the merchant district. The echoes double up on themselves, sounding nearer and then far away.

"Raaa-chel!" he calls, "Rachel, I love you!"

OVER THE TOP

There is an incredible series of explosions, the sound of distant guns. He is running through the mud of Passchendaele. A bullet has shattered his foot, but the rum, the giddiness of the fight have taken over his mind, and adrenalin has taken over his body. He drives through the battlefield, thrown off balance, slowed certainly by the wound, but running, always running.

Ahead of him is the brighter red of the earth around the enemy trenches. They are running back and forth.

Panic. They know he is going to kill them.

Kill them all.

He has learned how to work with the wound!

He finds that if he holds the rifle differently that he can take some of the weight off his foot. He can feel the blood soaking through his trousers as the fabric wicks it up. The artery pulses and pain begins to course all the way up his thigh.

In the trench just ahead one enemy soldier turns and cannot find a weapon. When the soldier turns again Forrest sees that it is a woman and she has been surprised in the act of dressing. Her uniform shirt is open and her breasts are heaving in time to the crash of the shells which are now shrieking louder and closer.

The shells may kill them both!

Fear overcomes all decency and inhibition and he collapses upon her in the mucky bottom of the trench. Her white hair fills his face.

"Ohhh . . . . " comes a voice.

An artillery shell has landed and the trench seems to turn sideways.

He presses himself into her and there is a deep kicking sensation in his penis.

"Ohhhhh . . . " and now he digs his fingernails into her arms as they are lifted and then fall through the air, turning so that she is above him. Her eyes are half-open, her silver hair flying as her helmet is lifted off and then the dirt—yards and yards of it—comes crashing down, pushing them even closer together.

Her chin bangs against his chest—

"Ahhhh . . . . " A last contraction in his scrotum, and then darkness.

She is terrified.

Now her arms are about him, squeezing. She is never going to let him out of her grip. Her chin presses even harder into his collarbone. Her boots are rough and are biting into the backs of his legs. The weight of the dirt is too much. They are both groaning and Forrest is beginning to lose consciousness from the excitement and the lack of oxygen.

The earth seems to tremble and he can hear a great motor. *Tanks!* The bastards have tanks. With his last gasp Forrest tries to manoeuver the wooden stock of the rifle so that it presses out against the walls of the trench and then, still locked in her embrace, he sinks towards unconsciousness.

END OVER END

Do you see the garbage trucks as they travel along through the city?

They're everywhere. Around and through the great clover leaves, past the skyscrapers, the light industrial areas, the heavy industrial areas, residential areas, mixed residential and business districts.

They drive past the schools, past the condominiums. Past the scummy downtown hotels. Past the parks.

They drive through places where the high-rollers live, and then they drive across the tracks where nobody lives.

When it's all done they drive through the outskirts—to the great sprawling municipal dump.

All day, all night, all year—they pull up to the edge of the gargantuan landfill, wheezing into reverse gear and hydraulically discharging their loads . . . .

And now, almost regaining his senses as the waste expands all around him, as the oxygen rushes in, Forrest is falling. Part of a great wad of garbage which tumbles down the steep slope . . . turning end over end—

A bad and dangerous fall.

Is he dead?

HITTING BOTTOM

A grey rain is falling, and he sits up, still in a stupor. There is the strong smell of feces and he realizes that he has defecated in his trousers.

"Shit . . . ahh, *fuck!*" Forrest moans and eases himself down into the mud with one arm. His side is in a puddle and he tries to roll out of it, but something sharp digs into the top of his leg. Already exhausted he rolls the other way, slips and his face slides into the muck.

"Goddamn! Fuck, fuck, *fucking* . . . . "

After a moment he realizes that it is raining on him. He gets to his hands and knees and pulls himself to the edge of the puddle which has become surprisingly deep, a *huge* puddle.

Forrest rests there on his stomach and looks around at the towering wall of garbage just in front of him. Birds are wheeling and diving at the top of the bank—an incredible distance above him; a hundred yards. Maybe more.

He falls over and looks beside him along a high ridge of garbage that extends as far as he can see.

"Oh, God . . . jesus . . . aahhh . . . . " Forrest gasps into the mud as he rolls over, quicker now—and that direction too, a long advancing bank of garbage curls around him.

Forrest turns and looks behind him.

There is a tangled vista of what can only be described as a flatland pierced by random clumps of ancient garbage. Ahead of him in the marshy bottom of the dump are a cluster of municipal workers' carts, great vans of metal that sit rusting in the weeds. Portions of the sides of the bodies of the vans have been ripped by acetylene torches for scrap metal, parts cannibalized for newer projects.

In the distance a long ridge of rusted school buses, their

metal too oxidized to be of value, hold steadfast against the advance of the bank. Above them a neon green garbage truck slowly excretes a ten ton bale that tumbles down the face of the bank, splitting into smaller lumps as it crashes down the incline. Above it the seagulls whirl.

"Goddamn . . . . "

Forrest lets himself fall back into the mud. Toward the bottom of the valley through a knot of broken windshields, there are a series of large concrete disks—thirty ton monsters that are slowly sinking into the muck. Who knows what they are for? There are weeds, some small mountains of gyprock, and a cluster of bathtubs that show various shades of pastel through the marsh grass.

After a few feet of crawling and dealing with a cramp deep in his bowels that causes him to fall head first into the mud while he braces himself against the spasms, Forrest realizes that he is at the bottom of the garbage dump, about as low as a human being can go. Even worse than the drunk tank. He begins to sob as the cramps pulse through him.

As soon as his insides allow him to get to his knees, Forrest begins to climb up the sides of the pit. He gets about ten feet and begins to slip back on the stuff. He lands hard in some sheet metal.

How is he supposed to get a footing in this . . . .

Goddamn! Shit!

He gets a few meters up the side of the bank, slips a last time, and lands in a puddle full of grotesque things.

He takes his hand out of the water. There is what he at first thinks is a child's balloon stuck around his hand, but when he moves to take it off he sees it is a dead condom hanging off his fingers. Forrest looks at it for a long moment and then, shivering, waves his hand back and forth until it falls.

He sits in the puddle, hungover, and stunned by the depths of his own depression. He realizes that he is crying—crying like a little boy, and collapses in misery and humiliation onto the lip of the puddle. Perhaps later, if he can get it together he can figure out some way to kill himself.

From where he sprawls in the mud it seems like a good idea.

A USEFUL TOOL!

The sky hangs darkly overhead. The gnaw of hunger and the nearby smashing of a huge bale of garbage bring him back to consciousness.

Forrest painfully gets to his feet and wanders to higher ground in search of a rope, some pills, a sharp piece of glass. Anything.

The rain has stopped completely, but the sky is still overcast. Perhaps smoke. Somewhere down the wall there is smoke. The seagulls are plummeting toward a new bale which lies just on the edge of a large pool.

Forrest shuffles along the rim of the pool until he gets to the face of the wall. The great sheets of garbage have spilled out of the compacted bale, and where the faces have parted the gulls are attracted, fighting each other over their treasure.

He wanders over to get a closer look at the great blocks. The gulls are tearing open the green face of a garbage bag. Chicken bones and french fries.

In seconds the bag is pierced and the contents start to ooze forward as the bale continues to expand. Some plastic forks and a packet of artificial sweetener fall at his feet.

"Fuck off," he mutters to the gulls as he steps closer to the bale.

He reaches out and takes a french fry. Recent.

Not bad. The gulls have all the chicken bones. Behind him, perhaps a hundred meters, is a low crashing sound and the rising call of another flock of gulls. He turns in time to see a second huge bale settle into place. At a greater distance, perhaps half a mile, an orange vehicle backs up to the lip of the dump and prepares to excrete a third load.

He looks back into the leaves of the bale nearest him.

Taco chips mingled with disposable diapers. In a few

moments he finds several other portions of fast food that have been thrown away. Most of it is less than twenty-four hours old, virtually none older than a week.

Forrest eats for a few moments and then the saltiness of the pizza crusts make him think of water.

Water—a much harder commodity to find!

You can't drink from the puddles! Could be anything, poison, chemicals in that.

Forrest scurries around the edge of the lip looking for clean puddles. They all have stuff floating in them or the rainbow shine of toxicity.

Well, there might not be water, but there are plenty of soft drinks. All kinds of pop. Most of the glass bottles are smashed by the pressure of the compactors, but there are many plastic soft drink containers which are flattened and unpunctured so that a few ounces of fluid remain.

The pause that refreshes!

❖

There is a scrabbling sound. A rattling of tin cans and a few grunts. Forrest scuttles along the edge of the wastefall scavenging breakfast.

His stomach has been full, and then a wave of nausea has emptied it again. Still the hunger has driven him to acquire a second breakfast, although the timing is all off. Looking up he has decided that it is approaching night.

He ambles along the wall of garbage now, skirting around the huge puddles that sometimes lap up to the edges of the trash. In just a few hours he has found plenty of his favorite foods to eat. There is no need to look in *every* can, he simply heads along the edge of the garbage glacier and watches the gulls above.

From time to time there is a rumbling up on the lip of the glacier. The trucks come, a huge bale tumbles down the slope, and, if it makes it all the way down, Forrest inspects it, takes what he wants and leaves the rest to the gulls.

Not bad, not too shabby.

Forrest pokes through the garbage with the toe of his shoe. There is something long and shining. He bends and gives it a tug and it separates from the wad of waste with a slurping sound that splits open the bale.

A barbecue spatula.

A useful tool! Using the spatula he can probe without bending, stab a convenient apple, bring it to his nose for inspection, fling it aside if it offends him.

Turning through his fourth bale of the afternoon he finds a liquor bottle that has been flattened, only the glue of the labels holding the broken glass together. He looks at it sadly, reminded of this problem which he will have to solve, casts it aside, moves on. Life without booze? His stomach rolls over again and he rests against the side of the bale and tries to hold in his second breakfast.

ABOVE AND BELOW

Life after booze. Is such a thing possible? There is a rumble from above.

He belches, once, twice. Sits on the edge of a wad, gets his bearings and finally stands. Above him is a growing roaring sound. He has heard it all morning long, sometimes louder, sometimes just barely there, fading in and out under the yips of the gulls. He looks up to the top of the wall. There is nothing. The roaring grows in power, closer now.

Above him one of the huge Caterpillar bulldozers is collating several tons of garbage in a line. The driver's mission is to 'clean up the edge' of the wall. There is everything mixed into this load— paper, plastic, household trash, a couple of water heaters.

Now the driver moves his levers, the monster machine twists its treads and jerks forward, blade down.

The driver wears a gas mask and goggles. Union regulations. The blade bites into the mounds of waste and grinds forward, pushing it and turning it all over on itself, forming the garbage into a rolling mass as it arrives at the edge and begins to tumble.

A long rolling wave of waste, fifteen feet high, washes over and falls down into the valley.

Forrest becomes aware of what is going to happen but begins to run the wrong way. The wave is advancing down the hill and will be on him in moments. At the last second he turns and runs away from the wall, trips immediately on some coils of wire, and goes down.

The wave of garbage washes over him, sour smelling, gooey, sharp edges cutting into him.

He stands dripping household waste and wades out of the

garbage. The dust makes him cough for several minutes, then he vomits.

Have to watch out for that, he thinks.

He looks at his clothes, even more completely ruined. A long rip in the trousers, the fly, (goddamned fly!) hanging open again. Shirt is stained and torn. Tie is gone. Lost. A fucking mess, Jesus . . . . High above him he hears the rumbling again.

❖

All day he has been avoiding the garbage slides. For some minutes there has been the low repeated rumbling up above him. Now a wave is tumbling down, heading for him, and he must hurry back out into the bog away from the bottom of the wall as the wave of garbage strikes and hurls fragments into the air. An abandoned hot water heater smashes into the ground where he had been standing and bounces thirty feet into the air, twisting end over end and then slamming down into the muck just a few feet from where he now stands.

You could die out here!

If he hadn't seen it he could have been crushed! Killed by a falling hot water heater.

All right, enough of this shit.

He figures to climb up the sides, but when he tries it he can only get so far. The sides of the wall become steep and with every step he slides back two. The ground is not safe, either. The wall is made up of jagged metal, old boards with nails in them, discarded shingles, glass, all kinds of hazards. None of it is stable. He slides down to the base of the wall, only just managing to keep his balance. No, climbing out is not the answer. Maybe with ropes of some kind or poles he could jam down into the mass of garbage to give him handholds . . . .

Christ, there must be some kind of way out of here!

He turns and looks out to where the towers of concrete are. Maybe if he went out to them he could climb up high and see where there is a—a what? A *road* that comes down into the valley? A set of *stairs?*

Fuck . . . .

It's time to get back to the real world here.

Up the line of the wall it is getting dark. Yes, almost night, he is sure of it now. Find somewhere to sleep, and then find a way out of here. Escape and get back to the real world.

Forrest beds down in a culvert made softer by the addition of what appears to be thousands of discarded service station flags.

Even in the night is the roaring of the Caterpillars.

THERE USED TO BE SOMETHING HERE

After breakfast he sets out.

His head is throbbing and his throat is raw. Everywhere now, as he moves along the wall, he searches for alcohol. After several hours all he can find is a single half full beer can. He hungrily drains the can, spits a cigarette butt out that was floating in the bottom and nearly retches. It's over soon. A warm glow is spreading through his stomach, not enough to calm him down, not totally satisfying, but it's something, isn't it? It's better than nothing.

He continues his exploration.

The dump is huge. It is an immense swampy area near a coast or coastal plain. Around the area the garbage, toxicity, and destruction of three municipalities converge. He has plenty of room, no doubt about that.

Every so often he tests the sides, not completely abandoning the notion of simply climbing out. The sides of the mountains of garbage are invariably steep and giving way. Crumbling into the bog.

As was the case the day before, his most important need is to slake his thirst. There are plenty of puddles, but the 'water' that is pooled there is completely opaque. All sorts of things float on he surface. The sheen of oil products makes rainbow patterns across most of the pools and puddles.

No way is he going to drink that shit, he figures. He scavenges for half filled soft drinks.

From time to time where the ground slopes there are creeks that flow beneath the wall. They meander out into the bog, heading for the sea. Maybe he could build a raft? Sail out around the entire area, get back that way?

Where the creeks meet up there are canyons, peninsulas of garbage. Areas where fires can smoulder. He comes to a set of huge sewer pipes that empty into the sea. Here the ground is steep and the creek has become a river, perhaps forty feet wide, slowly running toward the ocean.

Unable to cross the river easily without climbing up the garbage wall, and picking his way over the cement culverts, he decides to follow the river toward the sea as far as he can. It splits into a delta of half-processed sewage and then in the distance he can hear the quiet lapping of the surf.

There are the remains of an ancient pier. Not far away a forest of pilings. The litter of industry projects up through the sand, as the tide rushes over it.

There used to be something here once, he thinks. Listlessly, with no other choice, he turns back.

Toward what he decides must be north, the wall seems to project to the edge of the sea itself, making a barrier around which he could only sail (if he knew how to sail!).

But before that he would have to get across miles of swamp.

To the south, the wall stretches endlessly.

That's it. These are the limits of his world.

LOOT

Forrest develops a policy, a system of exploration and survey of the realm. He goes out each morning, gets food, tries to find something decent to drink and saves it *all* in a huge glass bottle, probably a carboy from an office water cooler. The water bottle is too heavy to carry on his daily wanderings so it acts as a magnet for him. He makes day trips along the wall and then returns to the water cooler at night, pours his collected fluids inside, and beds down on a collapsed sofa that he has dragged away from the active face of the wall down a twisting canyon of garbage that is a little more sheltered from the wind.

Home.

A few days later he finds an even better site for his 'headquarters.' It is in another canyon that lies bounded by a collection of abandoned vehicles and the garbage wall. There are maybe fifty hulks of automobiles there. The largest is a Cadillac limousine. Complete with bar. The seats are dry and wide and the car sits level on the ground. A roof over his head.

Lying there at night he watches the stars out the shattered rear window of the old Cadillac.

❖

There is no lack of communication from the outside world. As he strolls through the gullies and rills of the dump he would have to consciously work not to read the news. Each area of the city has a different garbage day, so nearly fresh newspapers fall to his feet each day. At most a day late. It is possible to follow the local, national and municipal affairs. He is almost aware, without really thinking about it, what motion pictures will be playing this weekend.

His home is growing.

A 'wall' of shelves has grown up beside the Cadillac. A discarded table sits near the front door. In one long day of supreme effort he has manhandled the heavy carboy down the wall to this new location. It rests on the table, fitted now with a neoprene hose, culled from an interesting fall of medical waste. A haemostat clamps it off, and he refills it daily.

Rainwater drains from several sheets of plastic into hubcaps. Now he can linger in bed. The daily emergency to find water seems to be solved.

The news carries the usual strange events: murders, accidents, threats of war.

One day as he combs through a recently fallen bale he reaches out with the spatula to puncture a garbage bag and packets of money spill out! All denominations.

He twists the tines of the spatula and the hole grows larger. More money! He scoops it up and does a quick counting when he gets back home. Stacks of fifties and hundreds. More than a hundred thousand dollars worth, and he didn't even look through the entire bag.

The money lies spread out across his mattress. He leans back and clutches a couple of packets to his chest. Falls asleep with the money blanketing him from the night breeze.

The next day he reads about the robbery in the papers. Leisurely Forrest reclaims the rest of the money, some bonds, all in three more garbage bags that are crushed in the bale.

Half a million.

He grows quiet around the money, conscious of its power. He ties the bags up and puts them in the trunk of the Cadillac where they will be out of the weather. And then in a burst of joy he raids one of the bags and rips off the bands around a stack of fifties. He pokes fifties onto every nail; finds invisible Scotch tape the next morning and returns home, tapes ten thousand dollars worth of fifties to the ceiling of the Cadillac above his bed. Tapes more to the inside of the front windshield where it will cut the morning sunlight that tends to stream in waking him too early.

And so he rests in the lap of luxury.

PRESTO!

Hell, you just cast it like that and if they're biting . . . .

(He is becoming a fisherman!)

He sets forth everyday to 'work' the slope of the wall for food and interesting items whether he needs to or not. He has developed a type of long, light ladder, made from plastic plumbing pipe; wire lashing the rungs onto a central pole that he can push up the banks.

Forrest climbs the ladder and casts, using a real bamboo pole, for any useful items that catch his eye. On some days he is lucky, on some days not so.

Surprising, wonderful finds: a cigar box with six nearly fresh Havana cigars. Why would someone throw those out? Did someone take the pledge? A wealthy man dead of a heart attack? He fingers the cigars experimentally. *Is it bad luck to smoke a dead man's cigar?*

In five minutes of looking around: matches.

Presto—a blue cloud of prosperous cigar smoke wreathes his head and Forrest strides along, looking, selecting, judging. Using his powers of criticism.

Everything is here. All the clothing he needs. The latest magazines, designer lighting fixtures. Cooking utensils.

With a second carboy he sets about to make a still. This is a process of trial and error because he cannot remember how the process of distilling works. It seems there are things that you are not supposed to do or else you'll go blind.

Having lived several weeks in the dump now with no alcohol he feels healthier, yes he does! But all the same it would be nice to have a drink now and then.

He improves his climbing system by weaving two ladders

together and using water ski rope to bind the structure together. Now he can forage up the bank to a considerable height. He still has to go slowly to prevent avalanches, but it opens another plateau to him, another source of revenue, and it also gets him that much closer to the top.

Never has he completely given up the idea of escape. There has to be a way out. The raft is a good idea, but he'd have to carry everything through the marsh from the wall. Take forever.

Going out over the wall is the obvious way. It would be impossible to carry or even make enough ladders to reach the lip, but using three perhaps, putting one or two down, taking the first one and putting it at the head, he could proceed slowly in stepwise fashion and make it to the top . . . .

But where would he sleep? He pushes that plan to the rear of his mind as he concentrates on building the still.

A carboy rests above some stacked bricks and is filled with a mixture of scavenged soft drinks and fruit fragments that he has gathered over the past few days. The bright sunlight has caused it to cloud up inside with condensation. When you touch your hand to the side it is warm, even at night. A bubbling froth has formed atop the mixture!

He pulls the plastic bags from the mouth of the bottle and is rewarded with the warm stinging vapor of success.

Yes!

And now every day—unbelievable finds, things that no sane person would ever throw away! What are they doing here, suddenly showing up on the end of his pole?

Marvelous things. A hammer.

A hammer! Wonderful. Now he doesn't have to use an awkward hunk of cast iron to make his walls. Now he can remove nails and recycle them with ease. Hacksaw blades, and finally a hacksaw itself. Several files and rasps.

He decides to extend his house to include a machine shop, perhaps a forge. If only someone would throw away an anvil . . . .

To improve his luck he decides that he will only drink on rainy days when it is no fun to work anyway. And he sticks to it!

The day he takes the pledge he finds a discarded drafting table, complete with T-square.

He roofs over the house with criss-crossed lumber and any steel pipes that he finds. When the bales tumble down and the force spreads out along the steel, the whole thing acts like a gigantic spring. Makes a hell of a racket, but it works!

Just outside the open end of the house are piles of bricks which will eventually become pillars to hold up the structure against the possibility of a direct hit.

PROTECTIVE STEPS

Every now and then Forrest wonders *why* this has all happened. If there is some *reason* that he—Forrest—of all people, should be the sole inhabitant of the dump.

And he marvels, fascinated that no one else is trying to live here. If they only knew!

Oh, it's not easy. It's no picnic. He works hard. You've got to be on your toes every minute of every hour. Escape is impossible. They're up there all night. Bright lights. Continuous dumping. Not only do you work to make it happen every day, but you work to keep it happening in the long term.

Yes, if they only knew, the homeless and the poor and the ones who just want to take the easy way out—they'd be down here like flies to shit.

There must be laws, he thinks. Laws against it!

Forrest begins to take elaborate protective steps to diffuse the smoke from his homemade stove. If, on any particular morning, the rumbling seems inordinately loud at the lip above his house, the stove is damped down until the bulldozers fall silent.

At night he worries that the house will somehow 'show' from the top of the lip, although it is an impossible distance. He checks his camouflaged roof daily when there is no rumbling.

He tries to think like the dump workers think. They must have some kind of . . . system . . . for the dump. They must put some things in some areas and some things in others. He knows they do this, he has seen piles of this, regions of that. Each municipality arranges its waste differently according to their own legislation, and three different ones use this dump!

Away to the north is the great wall of automobiles. They are dumped there and later reclaimed. Huge electromagnets lift them out into specially built crushers. There is even a railroad siding there and the cars go off to the steel factories and then come back as new cars.

Perfect! Forrest sits there watching it, smoking (for there are always cigarettes, always disposable lighters) and contemplating their reasons and whims.

If they found me . . . he thinks. Is there any law against living in a garbage dump?

Trespassing. You can get *shot* for trespassing. If someone comes on to your property you can just simply blow them away.

Watching one of the huge electromagnets deliver another automobile into the jaws of the compactor he suddenly feels threatened and retreats deeper into the shadows.

If they found out they'd bust him for sure. The house is completely against the building code. No sewer. That's a health violation right there. Trespassing, sanitation laws, Christ knows what else. They'd throw the book at him.

Then they'd find the money. They'd want to pin the robbery on someone, why not him? Why else would a person be living in a garbage dump unless they were on the run?

Suddenly the valley floor becomes foreboding. He even decides to stay in the shelter of the concrete rubble near the automobile ridge rather than risk being spotted as he walks home in the clear afternoon.

Farfetched? Sure . . . some bored crane operator is sitting there waiting for the crusher guys to get through squashing another Chevrolet and he looks away to pick his nose and spots something moving down there a mile away—"Why, it's a person! Hey, Bill! *There's somebody living down there!*"

Forrest, sweating now, squeezes back against the concrete. His hands unconsciously grip his pole a little tighter. *They're not going to get me.* He watches until darkness begins to fall and then he moves stealthily back home, eyes always on the rim.

Like a rat.

"PETE!"

Of course it's necessary to get a bead on what schemes they're developing, their plans for the dump. Are they going to fill in here first, or there? It could affect everything.

During the day, too afraid to venture out lest he be spotted from above, he begins to weave his latest in a series of ladders. These are long aluminum poles held together with woven garbage bags. They weigh nothing but support his entire weight.

The packsack goes around his back. A blanket to take the chill off during the climb. Some sandwiches, although he could probably forage for food on the way up. And then the rope. Miles of rope. The spikes are the heaviest. Who knows how many he'll need. It might be necessary to make a base camp like the sherpas do. Go up, make a camp, leave off some supplies, come back down, make more spikes, etc. Then complete the drive to the summit.

Camouflage. Never forget camouflage. His cape has newspapers pasted to it. A wide hat festooned with paper fragments. When he is lying on the slope he'll blend in perfectly.

The climb itself, when he begins, is excruciating. The ladders perform perfectly, and after each length a spike is pushed deep into the garbage pack. The rope gets tied off for a handhold and then he pulls the ladders together, pushes them out in front and that's another cycle.

But constant interruptions slow him down, and once a bale tumbles down the slope heading *directly* for his position, only bouncing wide at the last moment.

By afternoon he sees that he should alter his route across the fall line of the slope to hide in the shadow cast by the next ridge over, although this change will bring him under the observation of any truck drivers who do their dumping across the gorge. Still it will be an easier ascent and he can sleep there under the lee of the ridge, hidden by the shadows in the early part of the day.

The camouflaged cap is boiling! Who would think that newspapers could be so hot! His water is running out. He has lost track of the day. For some reason there is much activity on both slopes. He is forced to remain still while the gulls wheel around him. Slowly baking under the hot sun.

By the afternoon he knows he is defeated. He has begun to talk to himself in John Wayne voices:

"That's right, Pilgrim . . . " things like that. Slipping. He leaves the rest of the water and the remaining eight stakes. The base camp under the lee of the ridge is marked by some orange garbage bags tied to the last stake, and then he follows the ropes down, pushing his ladders ahead of him, shouting "Ho! Heyahh!" like a wagon master, slipping and tumbling occasionally, weak from thirst.

❖

Two weeks later he tries again. Climbing mostly at night when it is cooler. Stashing extra bottles of water high on the slope.

Gasping, he makes it to the edge and works his way around the huge mounds that are piled there.

What treasures! Here is trash before it has taken the hundred meter tumble to the bottom off the wall, unbent, unbroken. *Nearly virgin!*

He begins to circle the mounds that are collected near the edge of the dump, trying to remember what to take back—just tie it in a bundle and drag it down the hill.

The trucks come even in the night, lit by powerful mobile lights. Obviously there is some central control. Pile it here for a week, there for a week, sooner or later the bulldozers push it over the side. In some places there are ramps where the bales are pushed out the back of the trucks, and indeed, even as he watches a slow parade of trucks comes and goes.

Forrest sticks to the shadows, trying to remember the locations of the best objects, hiding behind the cones of garbage until the trucks pass him, then emerging.

He walks around one cone and sees a huge orange truck idling there. He edges around behind it and sees that it has excreted its load, but for some reason is sitting there. Waiting.

Driven by curiosity, Forrest approaches the truck, darting from cone to cone, hiding behind the husks of appliances that have been dropped off in a long row, lurking in the shadows of a pile of television cabinets.

"Goddamn!" something jerks in fear right beside him. Forrest, terrified, jumps back and throws his hands up.

"Stay away!" calls a fearful voice and simultaneously the person strikes him hard across the face.

Forrest falls to the ground but as he does so he grabs the person around the waist and is rewarded with a fresh series of blows on his back. The person's legs are jerked away.

"Help! Pete! Help!" calls a voice, high pitched, a woman screaming. The door of the trash compactor opens and there are footsteps.

"Over there!" calls the woman, and a flashlight beam cuts through the open portholes of the television sets.

Forrest *runs.*

Darting around the cones, completely lost. He sprints away from the lights. The sounds of radio traffic come to his ears. In the distance loud bellowing horns from the huge garbage trucks are hooting in the night.

Forrest makes the ledge and stumbles over the edge. In the distance dawn is breaking over the sliver of the sea coast—

And then he is rolling over, somersaulting out of control and desperately trying to brake his slide down the bank.

"Down there!" calls a distant voice as he falls, and a

flashlight beam cuts along the slope some distance away. Forrest tries to slide quietly.

Within minutes there is the sound of engines in the night and as Forrest hits the bottom of the bank, his hands and knees cut and bleeding from the fall, he sees the blinking lights of police helicopters winging down from the north.

He runs, *runs,* ducking into broken cement culverts, dashing along the muddy ditches where the sewer outflow has cut through the broken marshland. Behind him the entire rim is bright with flashing lights. Who was she? What was she doing out there in the dark?

A helicopter zooms by and Forrest resists every impulse and freezes until it passes, and then flops along the muddy ditch to a place where the water widens out into a pool.

There in the middle of the pool is a place where a great clutch of industrial refrigerators has been dumped. There are nooks and crannies between and under them. Around the base of the island weeds have grown around the jumble of appliances.

He looks aloft. Nothing.

With great long leaps he splashes through the waist deep water as behind him the sound of the helicopters' engines roar through the night.

I'll do anything . . . .

Did she think he was a rapist?

Anything!

Now a brightness is growing behind him, a spotlight getting nearer, shining on the water just across from him. He dives into the filthy slough, holding his breath.

Even with his eyes shut the light makes everything go brown, light brown, yellow, light yellow!

She must have thought he was going to kill her!

Please don't let them catch me!

"Haaaahggg!" He bursts through the water and arrives at

the bank, yanks his way up using the weeds as handholds and crawls desperately under the refrigerators.

Please!

PLEASE!

Pressing himself deeply into the back of a refrigerator, he realizes that this is no good as a hiding place, under it would be better. Above him the whirring of the helicopter engines seems to grow. There is another flare of searchlights, or is he just imagining this? It could be simply fear and the flash of light caused by his pressing his eyes together tightly.

What if they bring dogs!

He rolls out the door and crawls deeper into the appliances and then rests. Only a narrow triangle of light penetrates into this cave where he lies on his back. Finally breathing and—*there . . . above him!*

Her eyes seem to be anticipating a delicious pain. One immaculately lacquered fingernail touches the nipple of her breast which presses through the moist fabric of her bodice. Her other hand is lost between her legs. She stares at him, the ground seems to quake beneath him. Outside—the sound of the rotors rising—

Please!

"Uhhhh . . . " he hears a voice, realizing it is his own.

She smiles. Her hands move against her flesh. From somewhere else there are voices calling. Her lips are pursed as if to blow a kiss or say—

"Oooohhh . . . . "

He is aware of the pressure building in his penis, (to be caught like this!) And then her eyes slowly close, she seems to shiver, the fingernails rotate against the nipple—

"Aaaaahhh . . . . "

And it is over.

Prickles of light flash across her image.

For the first time Forrest realizes that she is taped onto the door of a refrigerator, the colours of the photograph preserved from the effects of rain and sunlight. How long has she been here waiting for this moment?

His breathing subsides. The sounds continue for hours and then gradually fade away. The helicopter has vanished. They will not find him.

Did he fall asleep?

"Thank you . . . " he whispers to her, and her lips purse in answer— She even trembles once more.

"Thank you . . . " he whispers again, and softly touches his finger to his lip and presses it to her paper cheek.

A MAN OF ACTION

When the bumpers will not come off the cars he has to use his acetylene torch. And this must be done at night for reasons of security.

There is an entire collection of faucets, fixtures for sinks and bathtubs. The bathtubs themselves, useful for the collection of rainwater. His system grows ever more perfect, depending on the effective use of plastic vapor barrier, castoff camping tents, raincoats, anything that will stretch and collect the rainwater.

The chrome is gathered into categories and arranged neatly along the curve of one of the gullies. Because the ground is sloping there and the parts shop is right at the crest of the hill he begins to call it 'High Street.'

Fearful that the sun will gleam on the chrome and give away his location he builds a roof, a sort of awning, and places the best examples in the front of the show windows so that they can be admired from the street.

When it's finished he steps back into the center of the street and admires the facade of the business.

Good.

Chrome, after all, is expensive. You plate the steel with copper first—that alone is expensive, then a layer of nickel, another precious material, and then lastly the chromium. The longer the electrical bath, the thicker the plating, the more expensive and rust resistant the piece.

He stands and watches the sculptures. Of course the automobile grilles are the most exciting. He looks at himself in the curved, surreal reflections. The beard getting longer, the clothes fitting him better now that he has lost a little weight from the exercise of building the parts shop. Strong. Successful. A man of action.

Oldsmobile.

Cadillac.

Buick.

Lovely, lovely works of art. Around the best grilles Forrest arranges a wreath of hubcaps. He sweeps up the sidewalk in front of the shop before he leaves.

A restaurant would be nice right here, he decides. Attract the office workers. A good menu, slow to change. Reliable food, fast service, low prices. Friendly waitresses.

You pull that off and the world will beat a pathway to your door.

BACK TO THE LAND

Finding a good handle for the rake is the hardest part, but before the winter hits he lays out his first field. For sometime now he has thought about a cash crop, something that would tide him over until the economy gets moving again. From the look of the weeds the soil seems productive, fed by years of organic and non-organic compost. It seems capable of producing almost anything!

He rakes the weeds away and levels out the field—the size of a tennis court. When he is finished he has a pile of bottle caps, broken glass and plastic scraps. He stands, sweaty and satisfied, already planning some sort of net to keep the crows away. The wind whips across the bog signaling the approach of the harsh winter. Perhaps next spring a second field beside this one. He will practice crop rotation and efficient composting. Turn this place into a garden of Eden.

Across the field he almost thinks he can see a willow tree, a picnic table underneath.

Nice place for coffee in the mornings.

THE GODDESS

The refrigerators have been moved. A block and tackle can accomplish anything. With a lever long enough and a fulcrum strong enough you can make a shrine worthy of her beauty.

The original fridge door is still there of course. Lit by a skylight. The scrap of paper now covered with a piece of purple brocade—it matches the purple of her eyes. In agreement he does not uncover this oldest photograph as he enlarges the room.

Now he combs the bales for magazines, searching for more images, and immediately is rewarded with additional poses.

She stands with her legs wide apart, the black high heels emphasizing the long muscle in her thighs, her perfect buttocks shining within the translucent grip of her undergarments. Her hair is black in this photograph, but he can still recognize her.

Carefully, he removes the staples from the magazine, moistens the photograph, and binds it around a piece of plastic culvert to dry in the sun. Later this pose—her arms raised over her head so that just the curve of her breast is seen from behind, glancing back at him, almost angry that she should be taken this way, from behind—later this pose is mounted beside the original.

Out of gratitude and careful to keep his agreement with her, he only visits the island on the days of the full moon, and accurately measuring this length of time takes much of his activity.

The last days leading up to the moon rising are taken up with culling the magazines for a suitable new image, going through a selection process, which can be surprisingly political, getting down to the finalists, making the *decision.*

Then, as the moon rises thick and yellow over the marsh, he dresses and makes the long walk, picking his way across the pool to the entrance of the cave. The lamps are prepared, the forbidden drink allowed. He places himself in an easy chair and quietly fixes this moon's photograph.

For the shortest night of the year, when the full moon floats high and cold, he covers himself with castaway sleeping bags and old fur coats and mounts a different version of her.

This one purchased from the Chrome Shop at an extravagant price.

Perfectly sculpted in the impervious chromium. She flies directly toward him with silver wings, the wind pushing her hair back in long flames. Her gown is pressed against her body from the force of the wind she embraces . . . .

As his breath becomes shorter—"Only the best . . . " he whispers.

ROLLS ROYCE

Heavy, cold and silver in his hand . . . .

WINDOWS OF ALL KINDS

He begins to collect glass to make a greenhouse. In his mind's eye he sees long rows of vegetables, certain special flowers—magic ones that are loathsome to insects. Shallow dishes of homemade beer to attract and eliminate the slugs that *will* come out the moment he plants the first seeds.

He acquires windows of all kinds, aluminum frame windows, rotting casement windows with most of the glass broken.

That's no problem! There's plenty of glass around.

A treasury of glass!

Glass of all colors, brown glass, blue glass. A bottle wall.

They pile up in cartloads the moment he grasps the idea. A little cheap cement and hey-ho, there you go.

Good insulation, too.

In the nights he rests in the Cadillac, now completely covered over with garbage, and muses on the enormous lessons he has learned while attempting to survive in the dump.

Insulation, that's one.

It's amazingly important. It's everything. The bottle wall will help the heating thing and help the light thing too.

For months now, as the tide of garbage slowly advances, gradually embracing his 'headquarters,' he has been thinking about a skylight.

Only this would have to be something more. A long shaft that would grow as the wall of garbage grew. Maybe a periscope shaped pipe, opened away from the garbage wall, towards the southeast. A gigantic light funnel that would beam some light into the Cadillac Room.

SEX!

The power of the sun!

All day long he harvests— radishes, lettuce, onions. Rabbit food. He has an incredible salad, the first really fresh food he has had in years. Homegrown and culled from the greenhouses that lie outside of town along the Coast Road, past the fields.

Belly full, farting, he takes the monthly selection to the island. Triumphant he enters the shrine, walking gingerly over the stones he has set just under water. (Invisible if you didn't know just where to look!)

He enters and opens up his envelope.

This moon's offering is an exquisite dark-eyed creature. She wears an undershirt that has been shrunk until it embraces every curve of her torso. She is touching herself already in desperation.

He places himself in the newly installed dentists' chair and allows himself the pleasure of her company.

A warm breeze infiltrates the shrine.

Old friends, she says, old friends make the best lovers.

The power of the moon!

AN EVENING OUT

"It's just here, darling."

"Ummm," she says.

As soon as she sees it she stops, amazed. Breathtaking. She almost giggles. And what is so wonderful about it is, not the decor, not the view, none of that, but the crowd.

What a scene! Even as they approach their table—*his* table, people are wanting to smile at her, wave to her, comment on her clothing.

It is fabulous for her, and they both know it.

The table is exquisite, by the window with a view of the shops along High Street and the mountains beyond.

She turns as she gets to the chair and gives him a look. *That look.* The one of promise. A look that says later he is going to be one happy fella in the big city.

Look at her! Grown sleek and cuddly with success and love. She may have put on a few pounds. To his eyes she is even more beautiful in this new guise.

The menu is full of foreign phrases, but his suggestions are absolutely right. The waiter is stiff, but completely correct and, because they have known each other for so long, he and Forrest, he retreats and lets them enjoy their time together.

"I've missed you . . . so much," he says sincerely.

"Me too . . . " she purrs.

"I feel that if I push . . . " and here he pauses, for the word has double meanings, triple meanings for both of them, "that you'll feel that I'm . . . using you."

Using.

She knows what that means, too.

The incredible eyelashes flicker slightly, she looks away, looks back. Gives him a sincere look, almost sad.

"When you're just *using* me, I'll tell you," she says.

"You know what I mean," he says.

"Maybe I like being used sometimes," and she extends her cool hand across the spotless tablecloth, takes his battered hand and kisses it with her full, soft lips.

OMENS AND ASSHOLES

On the day that he puts the light tubes in it begins to rain. The first of the winter rains that rise with the mist in the morning, starting with a toxic fog rolling in off the sea, carrying the hydrocarbons from the incinerators down the wall, the fumes from the maritime traffic out in the strait, the sickly smell of a house fire.

The rain falls black and cold and what has made it worse is that he has been unable to put any cement around the cardboard tubes because of rushing to get the bastards installed and the holes covered ahead of the storm.

Hard work. Shovel and spade work.

The new leggings work very well, the strips of metal save his shins a hundred cuts from sharp metal, rusty nails, glass, wire . . . .

And then, when it is all over, he goes in to check the angle.

He has been working outside all day and none of the lamps are lit, but already he can see the cool gray glow down at the back of the long room.

And now it is raining outside, so hard and fast with the thunder rolling in and snapping at the lip of the dump and puddling just outside the awning, but not a drop comes down the light tunnels.

Not a drop.

At first he dosen't think anything of it, but when the rain goes on for another three days and still no water comes in the two roof holes, he finds himself sitting in the Caddy and staring up at the tubes—waiting for the first drops that have to come, should have come already.

And never come.

When he remembers back he will realize that there were other signs. Other omens.

❖

One morning he wakes early, having slept fitfully, and stalks out into the Boulevard. His bladder explodes into the toilet across the road, and he shakes his heavy penis, pushes it back inside his robes, and goes off down toward the south, cruising for breakfast.

Bales are tumbling down in this area with some frequency and he begins to rip apart the nearest when a rustling sound comes to his ear. A knocking, almost a tapping.

Forrest scans the immediate area, but can see nothing. He pokes the spatula into the bale side and extracts a sheaf of garbage. He is riffling through the debris when he hears it again.

Animal?

He holds the spatula out in front of him and quietly moves around the bale.

Nothing. The bale has split open and a wad of material has spilled out onto the ground. His eye is caught by a large suitcase, quite handsome, and he goes to inspect this closer.

Real leather, and unbelievably there is the scrabbling sound again, emerging from the case!

Forrest fiddles with the immaculate brass catches and lifts the lid.

A baby.

A baby!

Blue and dehydrated and with just enough energy to cry as the colder air hits it.

Bastards! The shits! Who would do something like this! Fuck!

For several minutes Forrest stamps around shaking his

head and cursing at man's inhumanity to man. Then he realizes that the child needs warmth.

And food probably. How long has it been in there? The baby attempts to roll over. It kicks its legs and makes a croaking sound. The inside of the suitcase is wet with urine.

Reaching into the handsome luggage he lifts the little baby and tucks it in under his robe.

Shitheads!

The kid is dark, thick dark hair. A boy. Uncircumcised. Probably never even seen the inside of a hospital. The bastard child of some rich bitch, dumped into the trash at night?

Goddamn!

The child is making sucking noises and grasping at the inside of Forrest's shirt.

"Don't worry," he says to the child inside his coat. "Don't worry, you can stay down here with me." And he slings the expensive suitcase over his shoulder and heads back toward the Boulevard.

Assholes!

Where the hell is he going to get milk around here?

DIAPERS

A cozy place, warmed by the fire in back of the longhouse beside the Cadillac.

Lit by lanterns the child stares up at him with innocent eyes, absolutely focused on his face.

"That's an incredible turd you did there . . . that's amazing."

The diaper is full of long stringy yellow feces. He takes it and with one hand folds it and flips it into a flip-top garbage bucket.

He reaches into a bowl and with a wash rag wipes off the child's entire bottom.

"No more rash, no problem. Lookin' good on the front side . . . lookin' good on the back side."

Powder.

"Lookin' good!" He plops the diaper down and quickly pins it up.

"No problemo, señor!"

He used to hate kids. He used to go crazy if a kid cried in a restaurant, or if he went over to somebody's house and the kid was there, wanting *attention,* for chrissakes. Wanting to be noticed.

Used to hate that.

He puts the child down in the gigantic mattress/pen that he has added to the workshop. Inside are all kinds of trash toys, and mounds of bedding he has provided for the child.

He stacks another log on the fire and sits back in his favourite chair and watches as the child cuddles up in its nest.

Is it an illusion or is the kid growing already?

GRAVITY

Together they stand on the broad rising edge of the pool, the main thoroughfare—High Street.

"You see this street?"

The child says nothing.

"This is a busy street. Cars, buses, trucks full of all kinds of stuff . . . speeding."

He drops into a half squat and points down to the bottom of the rise and then swoops around—

"Vroooooom! Speeding right up this street. But you know what?"

Big innocent eyes.

"We can walk right across this street and never get hit. Nothing will run over us. We can lie down—" Forrest does so. "And nothing will hurt us."

He gets up off the dirt and points up to the lop of the wall.

"You can't do that up there." He bends down and puts his face right near that of the kid.

"Up there you'd be dead. Dead in a fuckin' second. But here, we got everything we want. More than what we need."

And back face to face: "And nothing's ever going to hurt you down here."

The child looks at him for a minute and then lies down on the dirt.

"Vooomm," the child mutters, causing him to laugh.

"Vooooom!" the child calls louder, and then jerks into a fetal position and begins to howl with pain.

Then as abruptly the child stops and lies out on the ground again with his arms outstretched, staring at the sky.

"That's the sky. It goes straight up for a hundred miles, maybe two hundred miles at the very most. Outside of that there's no gravity. Anything you send up there is going to stay there."

For at least awhile.

"You can't breathe up there. No air, no clouds, no rain. Don't weigh anything either. Just float around."

Forrest puts his arms out like an airplane and begins to move in slow motion about the street.

"If you threw a baseball up there it would go forever, until it hit a star or something, maybe turned itself into a comet."

❖

Growing.

Kid is reading the names off the cars: Comet, Rabbit, Cougar, Parisienne, Mustang, Firefly.

He begins to assemble things in little piles that have the same names, the same associations. There is Comet cleanser, Comet cars, Comet drywall. There are stars and star shapes, the star emblem from Mercedes automobiles, stars emblazoned on the flag of the United States, gold stars that someone hands out to schoolchildren.

He rakes these garbage collections into little piles, categories that sometimes have no meanings that Forrest can figure out.

FUNNY

"People are horrible, horrible.

"They are capable of anything, anything at all. And sometimes the things they find funny! Have you ever been to the circus?"

The kid looks up at him with a blank expression.

"Circus?" he asks.

"It's a big tent. They have wild animals in there and they make them do tricks.

"Well, all the clowns in there when they are doing their jokes, its all kicking and hitting the other guy. Wham, a pie in the face. Right?"

"Right."

"So, this is funny? This is what humor is nowadays? You hurt somebody and it's a big laugh. Ha ha.

"Well, it's always been that way. Right back through history. The Romans use to put a guy inside a bull. A metal cow, had a little door in it. They'd stick some jerk in there and light a fire underneath it and now the guy inside is yelling and trying to get out, and the bellowing comes out and this was funny. The Romans thought this was funny. Very entertaining. The Romans loved it."

Embracing the boy he teaches him how to fish.

He shows him how to bring his arm back in a long swoop and toss out a hooked line to snag a wide piece of metal, a promising gladbag. Teaches him how to play the line, how to keep a gentle touch and even balance on the slippery side of the wall.

And—still silent—the kid takes to it, scrabbling all over the face of the wall by the age of three, retrieving colorful objects, avoiding the broken glass, the jagged can tops. And running, running like a little monkey up the ladders to help pull in the line.

He has never eaten so well as since the child has grown able to help him.

"Together we can do anything," he says to the quiet boy. "Any fucking thing."

He teaches the child to hunt and gather in the dump.

❖

"What the fuck is this?" He rips the papers away from the child. He holds aloft the Sunday magazine supplement from the newspaper. A photograph of a world leader is on the front cover, pictured in extreme close-up, nervous. Below in bright red letters the question is asked:

China?

"You see this?" he says to the child. "This is a newspaper. This has everything that happens (so they say!) printed in here.

"This is all bullshit. Lies. Most of it is advertisements." He turns to a page of fashion advertisements.

"Nobody looks like this." He turns another page and is rewarded with a fitness ad.

She is in shape and absolutely serious about it. She has on a pair of leotards and half of a t-shirt. She has been exercising and sweat has soaked through the t-shirt. Her legs and wrists are bound to a strange metallic contraption.

After a minute he turns to the child.

"Hardly any of this shit is real. You got to be careful. They'll get you believing anything they want.

"You have to take this shit with a grain of salt."

THE DEATH OF NUMBERS

When the child, curled inside his long tented wing of the longhouse, cannot sleep, Forrest tells him a story:

"One day all the numbers were taken away. And there was no more money, no more clocks, no more counting and amassing of wealth. There were no speed limits. Fast was just—fast. And no one knew what to do. There was no need for bankers, of course. The stock market fell with a crash. If people wanted something they took it or used it or borrowed it from their neighbor.

"Everyone had to depend, in fact, on their neighbors, everyone had to talk. There was no such thing as news. There were no current events in the way that people were used to them.

"Newspapers wouldn't come out every day, because there were no more dates. It was not even worthwhile to keep track of Monday, Tuesday, Wednesday, for there was no need to count.

"The weather became more important, and time was measured by the snows, the rains, by the heat of summer. People began to live again.

"It was fascinating. If someone wanted to they simply began to learn how to play the flute, to dance, to paint—they just began to do it. If people liked their paintings they would give them food. There was no point to giving anyone shelter because there were no addresses.

"Only places.

"People began to name things again. There were new words invented. New ideas.

"Of course, this was chaotic. Life became upsetting for some people. They were afraid of death, afraid everything would be taken away . . . like the numbers had been.

"A man came along and said they had to replace the numbers with something. It was becoming too important where you lived, whether you were from the good soil in the valley or the poor soil from the hills. Poverty did not vanish. Greed did not vanish, like the numbers had vanished.

"This man said that they must change themselves, inwardly. They must base their existence on something else entirely. Not upon external things, but internal things. That the very moment of living has value because there may not be a next moment. That each moment, that all the moments are one moment. The one single moment, the perfect moment. Do you understand?"

The kid has to think about it. But answers yes.

"But they kicked out this man. He was not profitable. No one could drink their anxieties away. They abolished him and he was banished, to roam . . . the . . . " Forrest looks around, scowling, "the . . . *prairies* of this cursed world.

"They kicked him out, but instead of bemoaning what he'd lost, he found a refuge, and more than that, a fortress! Yes! Bullets could go right through him! The policemen could not put their handcuffs on his wrists. There was nothing there!"

Forrest turns to see if the story has made an impact.

The kid has gone to sleep.

WORK WILL MAKE YOU FREE

"The first thing you do is come in and punch in. That lets them know that you're there on time and you're not late, and whenever you leave if you have to go to the doctor. You get paid by the hour, right?"

The child just looks at him. The child is dressed in a miniature work uniform that the man has created. A long blacksmith's apron.

"Okay. Then you put on your safety equipment. That's in your locker."

Across on the side of the wall there is a 'locker' that the man has created out of a broken air conditioning unit.

"Then you go to your work station . . . . " Arrayed there are several crates and packing cartons with various types of hardware fastened to or hanging from them.

"Turn on the machine. You have to touch this button here."

At first the child cannot find the button because it is not a button at all, but a red painted spot on the side of the packing crate.

"Okay, the machine's going now. Put your piece in."

Beside the machine are several aluminum cans. The man guides the child's hand over to the garbage bag full of cans and helps him place a can on its side on a block of steel.

"Pull the lever—" The child does so and a block of metal comes down on the aluminum beer can and squeezes it.

"Harder—" The can deforms and flattens.

"All the way down!" The child leans on the lever with both arms.

"Good. Okay, take it out. Raise up the lever—"

The child does so.

"Take it out, put it in this bag over here."

Forrest is smiling at him. "That's your first one. Okay, take out another one. Do it all over again."

After a few tries the child gets it right. The man moves over to his own machine and begins to press the cans in a brisk efficient way, clearly trying to be a role model for the child who is attempting to work harder and increase his turnout of cans.

"We're cooking now," says Forrest.

They work like that for hours; the child goes through seven bags of cans. Forrest realizes that they will finish before the working day is done.

"Good, good," he murmurs and turns his machine off. Looking around for something to do, he finds a broom and begins to tidy up the shop floor.

The boy blows the sweat off his nose and tries to strike up a conversation, but Forrest stops him abruptly.

"Hey, button it up. You lose your concentration and do your hands wrong." He moves the can inside the press and places the child's hand atop the can. "And—*Bam!*—that's an industrial accident." He bends to put his face close to the boy's.

"No compensation."

When Forrest has his back turned the boy experiments to see if it's really possible to hurt his own hand in the can press.

"They couldn't stop me."

"They have ways."

"I'd shoot them."

"They'd shoot you first. There's more of them too. They're grown men, special troops. They have all kinds of things."

"I'd take all the money and pay other army guys to kill them dead."

"Take a lot of money."

"They couldn't stop me."

"What would you have anyway if you did have everything in the world?"

"I'd have everything."

"What good is it? It's just a pile of shit. Peoples dreams, illusions. It all ends up here anyway. You've already got all of it."

The child looks around.

"I'd do whatever I wanted to. I'd live way up high. A house in an airplane." The man laughs at how ridiculous this dream is.

"That's good, that's good, a house in an airplane."

"Anybody tried to stop me I drop bombs on them."

"Great."

"Couldn't stop me."

"They'd get other airplanes and shoot you down."

"I'd shoot them."

"They'd shoot you first. Put a missile right up your tailpipe." He laughs at his own joke. When he stops laughing the child has gone over to play by his pen. The fence is still there but it has been covered over by the child to make a cave.

A *private* cave.

TWIRLING

It's an annual holiday. One of the constellations is rising at the end of High Street. From a seat in the reviewing stand she and Forrest can see it quite clearly in the dark of the night, surely all the way over the horizon by ten o'clock.

The child is performing intricate manoeuvers with his staff in the center of the street. His costume is a splendid creation of red reflective material, almost like sequins that catch the light from the torches and send it sparkling into the crowd's eyes.

He stoops and hurls the staff toward the lip of the dump, twirling , twirling—and then catches it perfectly and begins to spin it round and round in his hands, an expression of deadly concentration on his face.

The man leans over to whisper in her ear: "He's exactly like you. Once he gets something in his hands he really can take it for a ride."

She laughs and squeezes his knee. She beams and applauds yet another stratospheric toss by the dazzling boy as he marches about the street.

The kid tosses the costume aside. "Next year I want white!" he says, and stalks off into his tent.

SECRET

As silently as possible the kid opens the forbidden magazines. Those are the ones—*the men in the suits.* Strange men with serious expressions. They are not like Forrest. The boy finds one photograph and studies it for a long moment. Hardly daring to breathe.

In the boy's hands a pair of surgical scissors begins to shape a piece of paper. Eventually a paper doll emerges. A piece of clothing. The front of a jacket. A trapezoid shape. Next is a triangle and with a piece of tape the child makes a lapel. Pockets.

By the time the sun is rising he has made a complete suit with pleated pants, a shirt, tie and suspenders. He folds it carefully and buries the materials and tools under his pillow. Outside there is a grey streak of morning light.

There are the sounds of the old man getting up and walking out to the toilet to piss.

❖

Atop a mound of trash the child shades his eyes and watches the contrails cut the sky. He moves to his own secret places in the dump and begins to cut out his *own* ideas from his *own* magazines.

There is a place that is phony. It has a broad flat painted yard that is as green as a billboard.

It is a lawn. A phony lawn.

There is a phony house at the far end of the lawn, with a door that is phony. He has seen these before. They look phony on the outside but they are real on the inside. You can see how the wood is sewn together. They do not last long.

But somehow the kid thinks the door in the picture could

last long. You could let the rain get at that door and it would hold up.

Are there real doors like that?

No, the kid thinks, that door is phony, too.

Is the sky behind it phony as well?

WHEEL

Numbers are numbers, Forrest says. Numbers aren't anything else. Numbers are only numbers but sometimes the numbers are not real. The numbers are bogus.

In this paper the numbers are totally bogus.

Everyday the numbers and the names change. The kid has begun to collect the pages and go day by day and watch the . . . listings.

Listings.

The names are names of monsters.

Forrest says the monsters have everything. They control everything. When Forrest says this he always looks up at the lip of the dump. The monsters are up there. They make the lines in the sky. They make the stars move, the little ones. The satellite ones. The monsters own them. They had them built.

They're only about the size of a trash can, Forrest says, and they have cameras in them.

❖

Using stones, fragments of cash registers, keys salvaged from the husks of broken computers, the kid begins to duplicate the workings of the listings that he studies in the newspapers. It gradually takes the form of a giant machine, a giant thinking roulette wheel, but more complicated. By adjusting the position of stones, bits of metal and springs, the boy can cause the wheel of the listings to react in different ways. He keeps meticulous records and is constantly improving the device, now grown as big as the back of a truck.

It takes hours to set up and Forrest rages at him for taking time off from work to fiddle with it.

"There's plenty to do around here, plenty of practical work to do without spinning that toy all day," he growls.

It is not phony though, and Forrest cannot understand it, thinks the kid.

The shop is phony, but this is not phony, thinks the kid, sweltering in the hot sun as he adjust a bit of metal that will duplicate the workings of one of the monsters' companies listed under AMEX.

Several hours later the boy lifts a latch that releases a spring.

The wheel whirls, numbers flash and slide. A series of tokens fall down a track, hit pins, pile up in a pyramid. Values are adjusted.

"Vroommmm!" says the kid, throwing up his arms to the setting sun.

WHILE SLEEPING

He is in the sky making lines. Behind him are great billows of new and fresh. He flies toward the walls of the monsters' cities and then wheels back at the last minute.

The monsters have hard clothes on that protect them but he pulls up his tail and shits on them.

Now they have a stain.

The child laughs and flies straight now at their wall. Their wall has thousands of squares and diamonds and hard glass angles to it.

But their wall is not a wall at all. He is not sure if Forrest knows this. He thinks that Forrest views their wall as one single wall that cannot be pierced, but the boy sees, *knows* that this is phony.

Because between the rectangles and glass that are obviously meant to dazzle the eye, to confuse—*behind that* are gaps—great spaces in the wall.

The boy suspects that their wall is really a series of islands, and that you could fly through all that and get to the monsters' homes with the lawns.

The boy flies through the towers and it is true—they are more like great sticks in the ground, shining like things from the dealerships on High Street.

But now, flying around them, the boy realizes why they are created so—for now he is lost. One side of the huge posts looks just like any other!

There are shapes and words on some of the tops of the posts, but these are confusing.

He sees troubled GazEx and the looming presence of Toys R Us.

He is growing very tired and the dazzle and confusion is beginning to hurt him. It is not easy to get to the lawns.

Fucking monsters . . . .

He uses his height to swoop low through the gaps between the glass posts and in the distance sees what looks like a huge puddle and a line of weeds.

There are tiny dazzles and housing values placed in among the weeds and he realizes that across the huge puddle are the homes of the monsters, but now his height is used up and he is too tired to cross the puddle . . . the gigantic puddle that guards them.

Lower and lower . . . .

SEASONS

Now the child wanders by the sewer outfall. Beyond him the jagged concrete struts, great rusting girders of a highway failure. Small trees have taken root beside the concrete and berries protected by the wind have begun to climb around the rebar.

It is dangerous and sharp, but when it is raining it is dry there and, within, a place where he has rested and left things he has found. Forrest has been there too and spent the night on his business travels.

It is a good place and here the child leans his head back against the cold concrete and makes his plans. Inside, wrapped in cloth, are his cut-outs.

It is almost Back-to-School and time for the new Fall Colours. He climbs to the top of the sloping piece of bridge and looks into a niche.

The Fall Colours—deep browns, reds, and dirt tones, are painted onto hard clothes that hold their shape even in the womens' dresses. The monsters place great value in holding their shape. Even Forrest says this. You don't want to get out of shape, he says. He even admits that he himself is out of shape.

The child looks at his robe. Like Forrest's it is in reality a huge blanket with a hole cut out for his head. Soft, not like the monster's Fall Colours.

He is out of shape, he thinks bitterly.

All Forrest really needs to get back in shape for Fall is some hard clothes. Would that make him happy as a clam?

THE PURPOSE

"All right. There's two kinds of every kind of animal. There's men and there's women. You and me are men. Well, I'm a man. You're still a kid."

"What's the difference?"

"There's no difference. You still don't have to shave and your voice hasn't changed."

"Will my voice change?"

"Oh yeah. It'll get deep like this." Forrest speaks with the exaggerated tones of an operatic bass.

"Anyway. Men and women, boys and girls . . . . " He stops for a moment, organizing his thoughts.

"Okay. Women, jesus . . . lets see here. Well, they are the ones that actually have the babies. They carry them for nine months and then go into labour."

"Labor?"

"Yeah, labour. That's what its called, hard work. Like shitting a watermelon."

"Labor sounds terrible."

"Oh yeah, it's awful, terrible. Takes hours, days, and sometimes they've got to do a caesarian, cut the baby right out of there." He stops, afraid of scaring the kid.

"Anyway, that doesn't have anything to do with anything, it's just that having babies is the, ah, *purpose* of the whole thing. So you got to remember that, all right?"

"This is a woman?" asks the boy, pointing to a photograph in a newspaper fragment.

"Yeah, that's a woman, and that's a woman right there, too. Those are young women. They're *models.*"

"Models."

"Yeah. That is an older woman. That's Margaret Thatcher. She runs England."

"She's a woman?"

"That's what they say. She's got a husband."

"Husband?"

"Somebody that lives with a woman for a long time. Maybe they have babies, have a house. Whatever."

Monsters, thinks the child.

"Anyway, it can get to be a lot of trouble. You wind up in court to divide everything up. Big problems."

"Is that a woman?"

"That's a *drawing* of a woman. Anyway, look, put that up. You don't need to know anything about that. All they're doing is trying to sell you stuff."

OLD

Everyday now his arms hurt. His legs are numb when he gets up from bed. It seems as if he is always on the edge of a cold and he had never been one for colds. Never got sick easily.

Now he tells the boy to go on ahead when he gets tired. He sits and procrastinates before taking on new projects.

High Street could use a sprucing up and the park has gone to seed. Well, the child doesn't like the park. It's too close. Nothing happening there except the gardens and gardens are only for old people and lovers.

He stands and looks out across to the plain to where the sea meets the wall. It must be a weekend. The automobiles are not being recycled. There is no smoke from the crane.

He turns to survey the house. It has grown long now, with rooms and hallways. Most of it completely insulated by the tons of garbage that have tumbled down and drifted up against the walls. Maybe three, four thousand square feet in this house. Something to be proud of.

He should extend the porch before the rains come. He should also venture to the south to check out the strange construction activity he can see high on the lip, and something neon orange that has crept down the wallside. Something is afoot down there.

The child is gone. Playing somewhere, he supposes.

He wanders out onto the street. Extremely quiet today. He turns to the south and peers toward the suspicious new development.

The faint sound of engines, what might be a curl of smoke high above the lip. Burning something?

At least three days to get down there. Have to be careful the way the wall is built out there; they will be able to see him for some distance.

Perhaps go in the winter when the days are shorter, but it would be too hard sleeping out in that weather. Too dangerous to send the child alone.

Later when the child has come back and is playing with his stones in the front room, the old man comes out.

"What the fuck is that down there anyway?" The kid barely looks up.

"It looks like a big worm," he says, arranging the pebbles.

And it's true, Forrest thinks, squinting. Perhaps like a big worm.

"Can you see that?"

"Yeah," says the kid. The old man tries again but only achieves a red-yellow blur.

"It could be," he says.

The kid laughs, "A worm that big, come on."

"Not a worm, but looks like one," says the man.

"That's what it looks like," says the kid. He stands up and looks down toward the south as if it's plain as day.

"You can see the sections in it."

Binoculars, thinks Forrest. I wish somebody would throw away some binoculars.

"Can't you see that?" asks the boy.

TEETH

"What are you doing?" asks the kid.

"Toothache," says the man, but his fingers are in his mouth.

"What?"

"I got a toothache."

"Did you lose something?" says the kid, laughing.

"Fuck off . . . . "

"Don't get your hand stuck in there."

"I got a bad tooth here."

"What?"

Forrest takes his hands out of his teeth. Blood and slobber are running down his chin. The boy makes a face.

"Are you a dentist?" asks the man.

"A what?"

"Do you know anything about teeth, have you been to medical school? Anybody that came down to Earth in a suitcase has got no business talking, all right?"

The boy just stares at him.

"I've got a really bad toothache here. I think I'm losing a tooth."

"If I find it I'll let you know."

"It's going to fall out," Forrest explains. The kid frowns.

"Jesus . . . . " He turns to the mirror and resumes digging in his cheek. The tooth has abscessed and is slippery. He cannot get a grip on it. When he pushes it seems to move around. It's all infected in his jaw. The gland under his cheek is hard as an acorn.

"Damn . . . . " He mutters around his fingers.

The idea of *old* begins to dawn on the child.

The idea of time.

CLARITY

Inspecting the strange worm down to the south will have to wait for spring, Forrest decides. He stares but sometimes cannot see it for the mist.

Perhaps he is going blind! Now he combs the trash and takes every optical thing he can find. He is particularly concerned with old eyeglasses. In one morning he finds four pairs. Three of them are womens' and the fourth is a bifocal with one lens missing.

He stands by the High Street and practices reading the sign on top of the Grand Hotel. Some of the lenses are better, but all of them are blurry.

"This doesn't clear up a goddamn thing," he mutters.

Over the next few weeks he dismantles cameras and comes back with a multitude of magnifying devices. Most of these are appropriated invisibly by the boy who is building some kind of lab in the back of his tent.

Strange, thinks the man, that I am just making a tunnel by covering things over and he is burrowing in the other direction.

Model 2, he decides to title his newest trial pair of glasses and takes the wire and plastic creation out into the street to test it.

Fine, fine. He turns to the south and . . . .

Worms! But now there are two of them!

"Hey!" he calls to the boy, "come look at this." There are two long bags, fabric bags that seem to be curling down from some sort of apparatus on the top of the wall. The bags are red with yellow lettering on the sides, and even with the glasses he cannot read it.

"They've had the other one down there for about a week now," says the boy in a bored voice.

"Why didn't you tell me?" he says reprimanding, almost frantic.

"You didn't ask, okay?" says the kid as he saunters off for the tent.

"You should tell me if you see something like that. Could be important." Somewhere under the tent the child laughs.

BEDSIDE MANNER

Resting on the wooden shelf beside the mirror so the boy can see it and learn from it, is a huge *tooth.*

A molar with a great filling and an even larger cavity that has eaten away almost all of one of the roots. There is still a fading blood stain on the wood surrounding it.

"Aaaaahhhh . . . . " moans the man. "Gimme that again . . . . " The child hands him a cold wash rag and Forrest puts it to his forehead. His cheek is grotesquely swollen.

"Try to find a doctor in this fucking place. Try to get to see a fucking doctor. And then, you know how much they'd charge? First there would be tests, then antibiotics . . . every fucking antibiotic in the book. Cost a fortune. You take so much of that shit that you're wrecked half the time. Kills all your natural bacterial friends. Kills the yogurt in your bowels."

"Yogurt?" says the kid. "That helps you stay in shape."

"Yeah, yogurt, tahini, all that shit.

"And if you don't go to this guy regularly," continues Forrest, "if you don't have a referral directly to him, hey . . . you could expire right there on the front steps. They don't care, man . . . . "

"Monsters," says the kid.

"Monsters," agrees Forrest. "Gimme that again, okay?"

When the fever gets worse at the end of the day the boy reads to him. The boy likes the stories from womens' magazines. Stories that are full of passion and tragedy.

"Don't fall for that shit, kid," moans Forrest after about the tenth story.

The kid watches him twitch in delirium. He worries, but there is nothing he can do. The kid goes out, gets food, water. Helps Forrest pee into a bucket, shit his watery shit into the toilet, empties out the bucket. Before he can get back Forrest is back in the sack shivering.

"You hear about people being sick, you hear they're sick and you don't think anything about it, but when *you* get sick you realize that you can't do anything if you're sick. You can't do nothing! If the Nazis came in here right now I couldn't lift a finger. I couldn't even run away. Just lay down and die."

"Nazis?" asks the boy.

"Ohhhh . . . . God, yeah. Nazis."

"What are Nazis?"

"Ancient history. War stuff, I told you all about that."

"Was that the Loud Man?"

"Hitler, yeah."

The child puts his finger under his nose and sticks one arm stiffly in the air.

"Are you going to die?" the kid asks suddenly.

"Huh . . . yeah, I'm going to die. Not right now, though. I hope not. I'm going to die, and you too. You're gonna die. Everybody dies. Everything dies."

"Is the Loud Man dead?"

"Oh yeah. He blew his brains out. That was years ago."

"So how could he come in here then?"

"Ahhhh . . . . Look, I just meant I was sick, okay?"

"I had a friend that was sick. He got so sick he died. He was my first real friend, and I knew him from when our mothers were in the hospital together. Some kind of rare disease. They never really found out what it was.

"When we were kids he always wanted to be Tarzan and I used to photograph him."

"What is Tarzan?"

"This guy that swung around the jungle and kept things safe for the lions and tigers and stuff. I'd take his picture while he was making Tarzan poses and shouting, 'ahhh-ee-ahhh!'"

"What's that?"

"Tarzan would call like that; he could talk to the animals. And we would play this stuff all the time. Later on when we grew up, he became a photographer and I started swinging. I was the one screaming and talking to animals, making the poses. He was running around taking pictures . . . I was climbing trees, talking to apes and shit . . . . "

"You're hot," says the kid, handing him the cold cloth.

The kid leaves Forrest and crawls into his tent . . . leans his head on the pillows and looks at the suitcase at the head of his bed

VUITTON

In a few minutes there is the faint sound of Forrest calling: "Ahhh-eee-ahhhhh!"

WORMS!

Now the glaze of ice has gone from even the smallest puddles and they set out, traveling early when the mists begin to form and the fog will cover them from the workers upside.

The boy rapidly runs ahead and Forrest walks along carefully, casting an eye on the garbage, adjusting his spectacles on his nose and keeping watch.

Both are cloaked in grey robes and the boy with a grey touque to hide the long dark hair.

They are in the oldest part of the dump. Vegetation has reclaimed much of the wall, the brown webs of kudzu and brambles climbing up almost to the lip.

Soon the child is out of sight along a row of ruined railroad passenger cars.

"Look at these," Forrest calls him back. The kid looks around warily.

"Looks dangerous to me," he says, poking at the rotten floorboards.

"Yeah, don't climb around in there." Forrest moves closer. "These are old ones. When they have that little ridge along the middle of the roof, they're real old."

"How old?"

"Maybe a hundred years."

"No way . . . . "

"Could be, damn near a hundred years. Railroad's all gone now, man. No more of that shit. They killed a nice way to travel. You used to be able to go everywhere in one of those. Pay for a ticket, go. They had bedrooms in there, dining rooms, restaurant cars, bar cars. Go anywhere in one of these . . . . " says Forrest.

"How do you make it go?"

"Need an engine for that."

"Engine? A motor?"

"Uh-huh."

"We've got motors, there are motors up by the cars. Lots of motors."

"Oh nah, not like that. Big ones, big as one of these passenger cars. Way back they had steam engines. We could maybe sleep in there tonight if you want."

"Dangerous," says the kid, giving the car another poke. And indeed the passenger cars are piled up on top of each other, stacked up like they had dropped from some giant's hand.

"There's another row back there."

These are a row of cabooses, some with wood sides that are lined up, truckless in the mud.

"Yeah," says the kid.

"Makes a shit to me," says Forrest.

They end up going on and Forrest tries to tell the story about the time he and his father—oh, so long ago!—took a ride in a boxcar from his hometown to—

"What's a boxcar?"

"It's a railroad car for carrying freight."

"Freight?"

"Cargo, supplies, food, whatever. Big, like those cars we saw today only with no windows."

"Why didn't you ride in one of the ones with windows?"

"I don't know. My dad just put me up on the side of the boxcar and we went for a ride down the tracks to the next town. Wasn't but nine miles. Real nice way to get around. They ended that, changed everything over to airplanes. Bullshit."

Monsters. Those fucking monsters again, thinks the child.

They watch the worms all morning long. The twin bags seem to be moving across the face of the wall. The 'mouth' of each worm is a large rubber bladder that seals the entrance so that air pressure can suck up any loose material. Paper, leaves, fabric, plastic.

Forrest and the boy watch it being sucked up all morning long. Then the worm always pauses and something is changed inside its stomach. The worm becomes stiffer, much less wormlike and sometimes the rubber bladder sealing off the mouth has to be adjusted from some unseen control station to keep the air pressure going.

But when this happens the worm is actually scratching at the surface of the wall, scraping away the first few inches of waste and lifting it up through the body of the long fabric tube.

"Conveyor belt inside there, some kind of machine in there."

All morning they watch it eating away at the wall.

Behind the huge complexes that are being built around the two worms a dark pile of gravel is growing, being spewed in high arcs from the two factories.

They move closer, hiding behind a low rise of discarded venetian blinds, millions of them that have long ago rusted and been overtaken by blackberries. Now they can even feel the breeze that rushes upwall to the rubber mouths of the worms.

"They're eating the wall up!" says the boy. His face is contorted with anger. Forrest has never seen him like this.

"Monsters!" the kid suddenly yells and rushes forward.

"Wait!" Forrest cries and jumps up and begins to run around the island of venetian blinds.

But the child is already at the base of the wall and climbing toward the lowest mouth, some sixty feet above him. He gets to the rubber bladder, has his robe catch under the lip of the mouth, but pulls it away, and then climbs up on the edge of the mouth, riding it as it slowly skims across the wall.

"Goddamn it, come back! Get off of there!" But even if the kid can hear Forrest he is not listening.

Climbing higher on the pulsing tube the kid reaches to get a handhold and then suddenly falls, striking the edge of the rubber seal and bouncing off, his prod being sucked away under the huge mouth as he tumbles down the wall and then finds his footing, perplexed and holding a metal box , turning it over and over as he runs back across to their hiding place.

"What's this?"

"Jesus fucking christ! Are you trying to get killed?" The child gives him a tolerant expression.

"No. What's this?"

"It's a video camera! Christ, if they saw you—come on, let's get out of here."

"They didn't see me, there's nobody there."

"They can see through these things. They can see you on t.v. There's always somebody there!"

❖

They do not stop to linger in the railroad cars but continue straight through the night with much argument from the child about the needless retreat. Eventually the child simply takes off.

Forrest stands in the darkness for awhile calling, but then quits. The child will be fine, probably back home already and indeed, at dawn when Forrest staggers in, he can hear the child's snoring coming from inside the tents.

He collapses in the Cadillac and falls asleep right away.

For the next week he keeps an eye on the worms, but there is nothing unusual. No patrols, no helicopters, no added security lighting.

Perhaps the child was right, maybe there was nobody there.

BLOW UP

The child is gone all afternoon. Probably out jerking around with his machine. But when Forrest checks he is not there. There is a great deal of smoke down to the south, and Forrest thinks he hears the sound of sirens on the wind.

When the kid comes home he is covered in soot, and pulls a long strip of neon PEOPLE'S RECYCLING fabric out of his shirt front.

"Where did you go?"

"I blew up a worm."

"What, what, what!"

"I blew it up with one of these." He ducks inside the tent and comes back with a bottle with liquid in it and a strip of cloth stuck down the mouth. Forrest jumps.

"I climbed up into the top of the lip and threw one into the room where the people change their clothes—that's where I got these," the kid flips a package of chocolate chip cookies onto the table. "And then I tossed another one down inside the worm." He smiles.

He is wearing a singed cap that says PEOPLE'S across the front.

"Listen, you're not to go down there unless I say it's okay. I don't want you fooling around down there, it's dangerous and besides—"

"I wasn't fooling around. You want them to eat everything?"

"Goddamn! That's not what I mean! I just mean that we've got to be careful. We've got a good set-up here and we don't want to blow it."

"Or blow it up," says the kid. He goes into the tent for awhile and then comes out with some stuff in a bag.

"Where are you going?" calls Forrest from where he frets in the rear of the Cadillac.

"Out," says the kid.

Where does he go? He goes to the ruins of the bridge where he has made his little place.

The next morning Forrest comes early and wakes him up. He tosses the bolt of fabric onto his face.

"What are you trying to do? Don't you think they'll try and find out who did it?" The kid just looks at him with those dark eyes.

"Don't you think they'll send out . . . inspectors, investigators, specialists. They have people who deal in this kind of shit all the time. You have no idea . . . . "

"Get out."

"Get out! You little shit!" He moves to strike the child, but he has suddenly vanished and is behind him, having somehow leapt completely around him, but now the kid is too confident, smirking. *Little shit.*

"Get down from there, you . . . . "

And now, red-faced, the child screams. "Fuck you, Forrest. I'm gone! I don't need you and I'm not afraid of them! Fuck you!"

And not even moving as Forrest takes a swat at him with his staff, taking the blow on his hip—*taking it,* hardly even flinching although it must have hurt—taking it and hopping over to the next huge girder and gone.

Forrest follows him out into the weeds.

"You're supposed to be in the shop in the morning. That's your job, boy."

The kid doesn't even look back. Forrest watches him go, so unlike him with those long legs, head down, away toward the bluffs where the worms are.

After promising himself that he will not try to find the boy he relents, even getting misty-eyed over the little shit's arrogance, blaming himself.

Guilt, blame. He wanders to the south, until the middle of the day. Finally, cold-jointed, he trudges through the wind which is beating briskly down from the sea blowing the paper scraps, fragments of plastic, leaves along the dump wall.

So in control. He seemed so in control and that is what is amazing, unusual to Forrest.

After warming up and the kid still not having returned, he walks over to the bridge and stands off a respectful hundred meters. Waits awhile, watches awhile and then calls.

Calls again.

No smoke.

❖

He sees the kid for the first time two days later.

He sees him high on the side of the wall, walking along casually from outcrop to outcrop.

"Look," the kid points to the south. "Three."

And indeed there are three worms! When the old man turns around to reply the kid is gone, vanished. Maybe just the faintest sound of laughter . . . a tin can rolling down the hill.

SLEEP WALK

Forrest wakes with wetness against his cheek. Cold, shivering and with his inevitably full bladder.

What is he doing outside? Fucking christ!

He sits up and realizes he has somehow crawled, been dragged outside the longhouse. He is lying in a puddle next to the Boulevard. People are looking at him from behind the wrought iron fence. How did he get here?

It was a tension filled night. He dreamed, but he is always dreaming now, of the worms, endlessly sucking. Three!

In the dream he is in the car, driving down the highway. Beside him the wall looms and for some reason the car, so long, so soft, lightly sailing from pothole to pothole as it speeds along the coast, will not respond to the steering wheel.

He changes lanes to avoid a bus full of tourists. It will not budge!

Cruise control?

Speeding now toward a bluff where the worms live—five now, and in different colors.

PEOPLE'S RECYCLING #1

In neon blue—slowly grazing on the bank.

He turns his gaze out to the sea and there are huge barges from the same company, the bright yellow letters and stick-man logo gleaming on the gray waves. Huge black hoses anchor the barge to the sea floor.

The Cadillac careers along treacherously close to the worms. Now there are smaller ones, some just a foot or two long, like snakes. And these snakes must have computerized brains because they can strike!

They react to specific bits of trash. Some go for bits of glass, some for tiny nails, bottlecaps.

Much quicker, slithering out of the way when he moves to brush them from his clothing.

They are eating at his clothing! He can feel them digging away at his trousers—horrible leeches trying to digest his pants, his skin—he screams.

And wakes up out in front of the house again.

People are clucking their tongues at him, and then respectfully continue their slow promenade along the Boulevard.

He limits himself to drinking on the cycle of the full moon. He walks wearily toward the island and stops there to watch the moonlight. The walking stones are visible now, the moat is drying out, the whole place is drying out. Greenhouse effect probably, he thinks.

He looks out toward the sea. A couple of distant plumes of smoke. Maybe it's the barges.

The moon begins its arc across the winter sky. He leans on the staff and takes another slow pull on his bottle.

What's the point of going to you anyway? You're determined to kill me or drive me crazy. Take the only thing I ever did right and . . . and . . . .

Trash it!

Forrest grieves and drinks, rages. And then calms down again. Never makes it to the shrine this time.

Too painful, too much work.

❖

Now he must make his own logs, collect his own food. He locks the bottle in the safe and heads north to gather supplies, and in doing this he finds the boy's house.

The kid is living up there in the garbage, on a higher level. Wintering there. It must be difficult. Maybe he is being frozen out and will have to come down. Forrest goes back and gets his ladders and the next day sets out and puts them up, calling to the kid first.

"I want to talk to you, man-to-man." No answer.

"You're old enough to listen to reason, you're smart and you've got your rights, certain rights that I shouldn't be taking away from you. I understand all that."

He stops, puffing at the top of the first ladder. He must be putting on weight. The ground is soft here and he is sinking in the wall. Above him, another ladder or two away, he sees the kid has piled all sorts of supplies, plenty of logs, bottles of water. The house looks snug and protected from bales.

And extra ladders, rope woven from bags, stakes.

"Looks like you've just about taken over this wall here." No answer.

There is a stirring inside and he sees the silhouette of the boy as he comes out to the lip of his burrow.

"There's no problem with your job, I've spoken to the boss . . . . " He begins attempting to warm him up with a joke, but then there is a hard snapping sound beside him and he looks up in time to see the boy pulling back a second time on a slingshot. Now there is another sharp sound in the garbage and something hard richochets off a cinder block and hits him in the chest.

A bolt! There is another snapping sound and he beings to back down the ladder, slipping on the old ropes.

"All right, all right!" He crawls down to the bottom.

"Okay, try to make it through the snow, try and make it up there. See if I give a shit." His chest is throbbing. He looks down and sees that the bolt has indeed torn the skin. No blood, but one hell of a bruise. He has done something to his foot.

Little shit. He hobbles along out of slingshot range and looks back up at the burrow.

The boy has gone.

GONE

Abandoned. Begging, pleading as he crosses the stones. Promises to maintain the moat, dredge it out so that the water will come back again. Open up the door and crawl in. Fresh oil for the lanterns and dry matches.

With shaking hands he gets them lit and then turns to the chair, easing himself down. Above and all around him she floats, now completely covering the ceiling and the walls in her many guises.

"Yes, it has been a long time," he murmurs.

"Too long," her multiple voices reply.

Some of the photographs are dangling from the ceiling. He had anticipated this and gently, (with shaking hands!) tapes them back into place.

From inside his shirt he extracts the mailing tube with her latest incarnation—so blonde, so perfect, so happy.

"I'm sorry, it was an emergency."

"I know."

"I'm sorry."

She smiles and moves against him and he begins to float away, to relax, remembering how he sat and watched the boy make his climb:

Working his way up by the ladders along the cover of the ridge, by Forrest's old route, and even staying overnight under the lee of the old freezer.

And in the morning, even with the aid of his telescope difficult to see through the mist, as the boy made it to the surface, stopping first and looking for trucks. And then—incredibly—hauling his suitcase up over the edge and walking away, walking away, not even turning around to give it one last look, but just . . . walking away—

And gone.

HOW LONG CAN YOU GRIEVE?

How long can you grieve? You can mull it over and stew it around and roll it back and forth in your mind until you have probed every permutation, every bump of error and second guessing, and there is still nothing to repair it.

You can wallow in as much self-pity as you can muster. And if you are lucky and grieving for someone you know has died or been shot in a liquor store holdup, then the event is over and you can wrap it up, eventually, in a tidy mental construct and get on with the rest of your life.

Forrest cannot do that. He only has the last image of the child, a silhouette vanishing, going down behind the lip of the dump, and no knowledge at all.

He worries of course, he worries. He invents scenarios, new fears. Occasionally the worms come, occasionally he finds himself rolling down hills to more hellish dumps, occasionally he visualizes the child, dead, sodomized, dismembered. He worries.

Not knowing is the worst.

And then when the ice is floating free in the puddles, when the mud is beginning to get soft on top, a newspaper sheet brushes past his hand.

He moves to shake it away, but it adheres. He removes it from around his wrist, and it unfurls and blows back to his hand again.

It is a page from a weekly real estate newspaper supplement. There is a photograph, a row of photos of agents, all smiling and promising fresh approaches. And in the center:

KID VUITTON

Salesperson of the Month

MILLIONS

Hoarding the newspapers, studying the market. The stack of clippings grows.

Forrest follows the real estate market as never before. A municipal map grows with pins charting the addresses of Kid Vuitton's properties.

Starving for information, Forrest collects everything. He knows Kid's business number, his work number, his pager number, his message service number, and his cellular number.

He follows the fortunes of the parent agency in trade articles that sometimes appear in the real estate papers.

There is an incredible amount of business out there, it is an invisible layer of . . . of . . . *commerce,* of traffic all over the world, over the city, the agricultural land, and the vacation real estate. A blanket of investment and speculation over everything.

And Vuitton is apparently good at it.

For several weeks as spring grows Kid Vuitton vanishes from the real estate pages, and then Forrest sees that he has begun to specialize in the commercial real estate market. No more house showings, no more finicky clients. And now the kid is dealing in larger sales, a million here, a million there—

A million! Two million!

Now Kid does not *share* a column with some other paunchy agent on the way down or some sharp woman on the way up. He has his own picture, his own column. Hair is longer, his expression different. He is in control.

In control of warehouses, small businesses, restaurants, franchise outlets, holding properties, for lease or sale.

Now the gulls wheel and dive as Forrest sits on the patio slowly musing through the business pages. Now the grass grows up around his feet and the sky is growing clearer. A moon will rise soon, he feels.

HE'S HOT

Of course it's the greenhouse effect. The heat. Incredible drought and pounding sun that keeps Forrest buried in the cool of his longhouse during the entire day.

He ventures out nearly naked except for his broad ancient camouflage hat or the hard gaiters that he knots around his bony legs when he has to reach into the wall for food.

The flowers are the first to go. Billions of them, a riot of colour growing wild in the hills throughout the dump. Taking root everywhere, with long stems that nod in the slightest breeze—now suddenly drying up, parched, burnt about the petals. Dried out before they can make their seeds.

All that's left in this elongated summer are the hard weeds, swamp flowers. Insects and wildlife that can't handle the heat and the lack of moisture, sicken and die, or attempt to adapt hideously.

Where are the frogs? Where are the mosquitoes? Where are the spiders? All burnt away, all waiting, like Forrest, in the cool darkness of the burrows.

❖

Kid has his own firm now, called KIDD VENTURES, LTD. Forrest has the address, the numbers. From time to time other men, and more often than not, women are hired or promoted by KIDD VENTURES. In the beginning they all have the same serious look as Kid had in his initial business portraits, but soon there comes a kind of lightness, a whimsy to the faces of some of his employees.

Kid is attracted to *any* expression of ethnicity! His employees and managers are often wearing turbans, saris, sarongs, caftans, fezzes.

In vain Forrest searches for more information, but apparently Kid is publicity-shy. He refuses to give interviews.

He's embarrassed by me, thinks Forrest with a sting deep in his heart. Ashamed to have been a child raised in the dump.

Now he's with *them* he's too good for the dump. Ungrateful.

"Sharper than a serpent's tooth," mutters Forrest under his breath. He places the papers in a stack, and watches the heat shimmer rising over the hard packed soil of the Boulevard.

It's the greenhouse effect.

THE KID AS MAN

Kid Vuitton's car pulls up to the edge of the curb and before the wheels have stopped the door is opened and Kid exits lightly, holding the door open for an absolutely stunning woman.

Motorized cameras whirr, strobe lights begin to flash. Kid holds her satin-gloved hand and they walk down the red carpet into the theatre for the awards ceremony.

She is only the latest. She knows it and so does Kid. He's young and attractive, considered a great catch. His hair is longer now.

Forrest finds him in the smartest magazines. Some starlet is suicidal because he won't return her calls. Her co-workers on the series are worried. Will they have to write her out? There are rumours of drugs and mental cruelty. Verbal abuse.

The tabloids are having a field day. Forrest can barely read them it is so disgusting.

Kid in sunglasses, Kid striking a photographer. Kid in court.

The starlets, the models, the singers. All are broken-hearted, all bitter.

KID KILLED MY BABY!

—scream the papers. Stories of bitter early morning beatings. Too much vodka. Kid is arrested for driving his vehicle in an intoxicated condition.

Now other men, curiously attracted to women that have once (twice, three times?) been with Kid are measuring themselves against him. These recycled starlets, models, heiresses are all much happier, intending to settle down. Everyone has matured and Kid can continue at his own pace without lawsuits, injunctions, and the hassles born of lust and jealousy.

❖

The leaves die and fall. The rains rain. The winds blow. It snows and Forrest is happy to see that Kid seems to be quietening his celebrity life and taking care of business. The holiday season approaches and no one wants to write or read about greed or finances.

Interest rates are rising again and Kid has to juggle things. Has he gone too fast? Is there about to be a restructuring?

Forrest paces up and down High Street, reading the Wall Street Journal from cover to cover trying to get a fix on the Kid.

Can he pull it off?

MEN IN HARD CLOTHES

In the darkness, his head pressed firmly against the door of the Cadillac, Forrest tosses, turns . . . .

Dreams.

He watches as the worms sweep the walls, watches as Kid's reproduced likeness, jowly and hidden behind tinted sunglasses, is swept up into the hissing worms.

KIDD SAN falls twenty points on the Tokyo exchange. The latest production from VUITTON-FOX is a bomb, losing multimillion dollar sums in fourteen hundred theatres over the first weekend.

There is a revolt of one of the boards of directors.

Men in hard clothes surround the boy. He is now only the child, dirty, his hair long and flying, still holding a bag of reclaimed aluminum cans in his dirty fist. Vainly Kid swings the bag of cans at the craven executives. But too quickly, outnumbered, he is forced to the edge of a tall office window—a spiderweb of cracks streak the tinted glass and the boy—screaming—falls . . . .

Forrest feels the wet against his cheek. Wakes up in a puddle almost completely across the Boulevard. It is snowing. His beard is white. He begins to cry.

THE RETURN

The dump is an ice wilderness, paralyzed by cold. Day is non-existent. Only a lightening of the grey sometime around noon. It is impossible to spot the rising moon, and Forrest would not venture from the warmth of the longhouse if he could.

A huge bale has tumbled down and destroyed the front awning, splitting into two huge halves that block traffic on the southbound lane of the Boulevard. It is impossible for the street crews to work in this weather, and who would have the nerve to ask them?

Forrest will not clean the bale away from the door, for it actually acts as a windbreak and keeps the longhouse that much warmer.

How can the summers be so hot and the winters this deep, this deathly cold?

Cold to the bone.

Forrest moves as little as possible. There is ample food and most of it stays frozen if placed far enough from the fire.

In the night comes a great roaring sound and from where Forrest rests, covered by blankets and garbage-bag quilts, inside the Cadillac, he can see the flare of searchlights sweeping the Boulevard.

The roaring grows into a shriek and drives him up and to the mouth of the longhouse, his staff clutched in his thin hands, knees shaking from fear and cold.

Outside at the intersection of the Boulevard and the Coast Road a shining, screaming helicopter turns and settles itself onto the frozen ground. The rotors turn slower and a door opens.

Kid lightly descends! He walks, head bowed slightly, out from under the turning blades and then toward Forrest.

"What do you want?" Forrest calls, too angrily.

"I don't want anything."

"Nice clothes," says Forrest. Kid is dressed in a classic tuxedo, patent leather shoes that are already scuffed from the uneven ground of the dump. Kid stops and surveys the man.

"I thought I'd check up and see if you were still alive."

"I'm alive."

"I wasn't sure."

"What do you want?"

"I already told you I don't want anything. I just wanted to see how you were."

"I already know how *you* are," sneers the old man. "It's pretty tough out there. You beginning to see what I meant?"

"It's not so tough," says Kid, smiling faintly.

"They're really starting to work you over at the Security and Exchange Commission I see," says Forrest, deliberately baiting.

"It doesn't matter."

"It doesn't matter? Haw haw! They're going to cut off your balls, you'll probably go to jail," crows the old man.

Kid just stands there looking at him.

"That make you happy?" he asks.

"It's what you deserve!" screams the old man, surprising himself. He'd really never thought about it.

"I thought you might want to go for a ride, maybe take a vacation from"—he looks around at the frozen dump—"all this."

"No. I don't want a vacation. I'm perfectly happy, and I don't need you or your fucking whirlybird to take me up if I want to go up!"

"Okay. Just a thought."

"You wanted to leave, what did you come back for, you wanted to leave so bad?"

Kid looks at him for a long time. Forrest actually thinks the expression on his face may be tinged with sadness.

"I just thought I'd check and see if you were dead or if you wanted to move somewhere else. All this stuff—" The kid looks around at the dump again, (wistfully?) "—all this stuff might change. Maybe sooner than you'd be ready for it. I just thought you might want to . . . leave for awhile." Kid turns and looks at him. "Forget it," he says. He begins to walk back.

"Take care of yourself," he says over his shoulder to Forrest.

"You take care of yourself," calls Forrest, following along behind him. He reaches out and grabs Kid's overcoat—amazingly soft in his hand. For a moment he is distracted. The coat is covered with some sort of rich fur—seal fur!

Forrest looks up into the perfectly sculpted face of the Kid. "You're the one's needing to take care of yourself. Stay away from the dancers. They'll kill you. Kill you! You don't have to parade around here in your fancy threads. I don't need any charity! I got everything, I got no problems."

"No . . . . " says Kid quietly.

He turns and smoothly walks back to the helicopter, climbs in the seat and puts on the helmet. He can fly it himself? He can actually fly one of those things . . . ?

The rotors speed up and Kid rises slowly, turning his tail rotor and banking off over the sea—vanishing into the blackened cold night.

Forrest watches the flashing red and green lights winking away over the wall and then gone . . . .

Gone.

It is very, very cold.

"I fuckin' told him," mutters Forrest and tosses the newspaper onto the fire.

VUITTON GETS TWO YEARS

Now he finds out what real life is like, thinks Forrest. Now he gets it up the ass from all the weirdo sadist jailbirds that are just waiting to divvy him up in the courtyard, in the showers. Poor little bastard.

The newspaper abruptly turns brown and then bursts into a yellow sheet of flame.

I fuckin' told him. You screw around with the tax boys and they'll nail your ass to the wall.

All afternoon Forrest muses about the unlucky deal of the cards that has gone Kid's way. Then comes another paper:

KID GETS OFF!
"I'm sorry" says Playboy Vuitton

Whoa! What's this? thinks Forrest and immediately starts digesting the news.

Ah-ha! It's the old community service ploy. Kid has pledged to devote at least sixty per cent of his business activities to 'socially redeeming' causes. This includes personal appearances, the setting up of special schools, and the conversion of a portion of his financial and stock holdings to investments that are more socially productive. Kid has also expressed a long withheld desire to "do something about the environment," as he puts it.

"Goddamn . . . " mutters an amazed Forrest, and he searches for the most recent business journals.

And lo, the plans are already underfoot! VUITTON RECLAMATION will immediately plunge heavily into all sorts of environmentally useful stocks. Toxic waste re-processing, waste removal, metal recycling.

Waste removal!

Within days a series of distant explosions cause Forrest to venture outside. Worms are closing in from the north now, only these are huge green ones, with multiple heads. He adjusts his spectacles—Model 7—and peers toward the car mountains.

Yes! Huge green worms, made of some other material, a silkier, shiny material that looks weather resistant. They graze across the snow covered wall leaving great gashes in the surface, the little heads going first, bristling with specialized robotic sorters.

And prominent on the side, white letters forty feet tall:

VUITT-REC #1

Of course! It was only natural. It had to be.

❖

In the days that follow, Forrest follows the fortunes of KIDD INDUSTRIES, KIDD CORP., KID-CO., VUITTON HOLDINGS, LTD., VUITTON REAL ESTATE, VUITTON-FOX (since reorganized into VUITTON ENTERTAINMENT), and VUITTON RECLAMATION.

Oh, what a strategy, what a vision! Forrest can see it all now, all *his* mistakes coming to fruition in the boy's twisted path amongst the monsters.

VUITTON RECLAMATION professes to first mine the dumps of the world, like everyone else is doing by now, but with a greater degree of efficiency and at a lower cost. That's the first advantage the kid has over the competition. He knows where to look. But it does not stop there.

The rights to develop the lands *beneath* the dump and any strata within, below, or even on top of the dump are gradually being acquired by KIDD CORP. They are licensed in a complicated four-way deal involving huge tax-free grants given by the federal government to actually reclaim this 'under-used' land.

It's a monster real estate grab—a mining operation and a monster real-estate grab rolled into one!

Forrest goes out to check. It is beyond belief.

KIDDSAFE INC., the toxic waste disposal company, is dumping its tankers into the sea to the south. Does anyone know? Does anyone care? No one seems to mind.

The smokestacks above the hulking worm complexes of VUITTON-RECs #1, #3, and #5 are higher and belch forth blacker smoke than either UNIVERSAL, PEOPLE's, or SONY's.

Where will it end?

❖

Is it being done out of hate? Should he have made peace with the Kid and gone for the helicopter ride? Would that have changed anything?

Forrest has a last aperitif in the Blue Room and gazes at the holiday traffic along High Street.

Christmas is always the worst time. Everyone pretending to be happy. It's all so, what's the word—ironic.

All those fools shopping for things they don't need, toys that the children will be bored with, shit that they'll give to friends they don't even like—they don't realize that the world as they know it is about to die! It's all going to be completely eradicated by the combined efforts of the Kid and his employees.

Eventually (and Forrest can see it now!) the entire street will be grazed flat by VUITTON-REC's; what can't be put back into production will be milled into tiny glass crystals, the dump leveled using laser survey technology, bulldozed flat and turned into 'useful' real-estate. *All of it,* the chrome shop, the plaza, the park, the fountains and sculptures up by the Grand Hotel—gone.

❖

To Forrest it is obvious. He should have known, he should have seen. He didn't. He screwed it up years ago. Why? How? Who knows.

The only way he could make up for it is to somehow stop the kid. Maybe he should get out and kidnap the kid. If that dosen't work, beat some sense into him, or anything. Maybe even . . . kill the boy?

Forrest lingers until most of the people have gone home. High Street is empty. Not even a policeman. The bus drivers are on holiday hours. Away over the University the moon is rising. He can see the lights of the worm complexes defining the rim of the wall.

Kill the boy?

IT DOES NOT

One by one the photographs peel away from the ceiling. Some crumble in his hands. A brassiere, an almost hairless crotch encased in blackest silk . . . .

A nipple, a leg. All of them come down and are piled respectfully on the seat of the dentist's chair. When he has done, occasionally sobbing for reasons which he cannot even begin to understand, he quietly pours the kerosene over the chair, soaking the clippings and photographs and, placing himself in the entrance, tosses a match onto the pile.

It does not erupt into flame.

It does not burst into an explosion of fumes and sparks.

He stands for several minutes as the kerosene catches slowly, creeping over the knees, the hair, the lingerie.

The plastic of the dentist's chair melts and the stuffing inside catches with a bright flame and now, coughing, Forrest backs out of the shrine, feeling the draft rushing in past him.

He pauses for a few moments outside, walks across the stepping stones and watches it all go up in oily black flames.

❖

There are still ladders piled against the burrow where the boy left them, there are still ropes and stakes. He waits until the weather is good, takes the time to fatten himself up, and carries enough food to make the journey.

It takes weeks to plan. The weather is bad and he must postpone the climb. He takes it as a sign.

He visits his burnt out shrine, and deposits another cache of photographs he has culled from recent magazines. He burns them, apologizes for the abuse and ill treatment she has received at his hands over the years.

Forrest stands at the entrance to the shrine as the magazines burn and thinks he hears her voice in the rushing of the draft as it blows inside and up the chimney.

"I loved you, I loved you, I loved you . . . ." He cannot be sure. He is no longer sure of what he knows, or doesn't know.

Forrest steps back, fingers burnt from the match he forgot to blow out, and casts an eye on the heavens.

It does not matter that the weather is turning. It does not matter about the preparations or the food.

It does not matter.

THE CLIMB

The dump is dying.

The sides of the wall give way in constant avalanches. Recently the rats have had a population explosion and become a real threat. The gulls react to his presence as an invader, an outsider. They swoop low to attack and disrupt as he moves slowly up the incline, a ladder at a time.

He stumbles, he falls. He scrapes his hand badly, a deep cut that begins to throb as the day wears on. The birds attack again and ruin his concentration. He often finds himself resting at the ends of the ladders, lost in thoughts of the boy, involved in remembered business disputes with cantankerous High Street merchants, or the unions in the garment district.

Then he seems to wake up and continues to plunge forward, upward, onward.

He uses his staff and a hook on a line. He pulls himself up using the hook, hoping it will hold, falling flat when it slips.

His feet make little wastefalls beneath the ladders, bottles and tin cans go clattering down the slope, dislodging others, a constant reshuffling of the wall beneath him.

Forrest falls. His white hair wisps over his eyes and he ends up going to sleep there, not even noticing the ladder itself slipping away down the slope behind him. Weak.

How many days is he there? He remembers nights where the stars almost seem to be joking with him, rearranging themselves into dot drawings of automobiles, chicken sandwiches, cold beer bottles. Stars shoot out of the drawings and drip down the neck of the star-bottles and onto the star-table. He sees her dancing, silver and starry in the heavens.

One great dagger of stars points across the horizon to the west—toward the lip of the dump, toward the lights of

VUITTON-REC #25 and whatever else has grown up there over the decades that he has been away.

It begins to rain. The wind whips at him as he lies there. Forrest slowly gets to his knees. One step at a time he crawls up the wall.

He begins to talk to the boy/storm.

"Forgive me. I screwed you up. I was trying to live out all the things I wanted and protect you and give you stuff I never had, opportunities, stuff like that . . . . "

There is no answer from the clouds which are boiling down on him.

"Listen to me! Goddamn it. There comes a time when you have to grow up, you have to realize what it's all about. I mean, it's not all about getting things, and toys, and material objects. It's not even all about love, or loving one person.

"It's not about winning, for chrissake. It's not about any of that. All that is shit.

"What it *is* about is here and now. And the way things are, just are in the universe. Doing unto others. That kind of stuff, laws, universal laws. Cosmic fucking laws! And you shouldn't fuck with them, Kid!"

It has begun to hail.

Forrest's hands slip on the shiny scrap metal. His knees quiver and shake and he has to spread his weight out to keep from sliding down and losing more ground than he makes during the climb.

"It's about being gentle and not . . . *altering* anything. It's about floating, and the beauty that you can find . . . . "

He slips and goes down hard into a garbage bag. The smell of sour milk and coffee grounds.

"It's about the simplicity of breakfast . . . good service . . . a menu that you can count on—aaaahhhh!"

His foot has found a hole in the wastefall and the knee is wrenched, painfully! Forrest falls backward, head down. His body is totally out of control. The rain is soaking him, his hands clutch feebly at the garbage around him.

"Listen . . . listen, goddammit. I made you. I'm your father, your real father. Listen to me. I just want . . . . " What does he want?

"I just want to tell you that I'm sorry, I'm sorry I screwed up the world so bad . . . I just don't want you to follow in my . . . aaaahhh!"

The waterlogged garbage slides away and Forrest's leg slips out of its hole. He manages to clutch the side of a rusting shopping cart and get to his knees.

His head is clearer from hanging upside down and he realizes with delight and surprise that he is just below the lip. A difficult climb to be sure, but he can do it. He almost *has* done it!

There is the snap of lightning off to the north. For a moment the air is suffused with the sweet smell of ozone. He begins to climb, stabbing his feet down into the soft garbage, sucking a foot out (losing a shoe!) but continuing.

"People don't have to make the same mistakes, over and over," he mutters. In the clouds he can see the boy's face staring at him. The thunder grows lower, rumbling, the sound of a huge jet engine.

Slurrp! In goes the leg . . . sloorrp! out comes the other one. A little higher.

"Don't let them do the same thing to you! Don't let them turn you into a monster! Rise above, rise above . . . . "

The roaring has grown so loud that Forrest is rigid with fear. Ahead of him a great steel box swells over the edge. Red taillights. Air brakes. The huge neon white letters glowing—

KIDD ENVIRONMENTAL

DISPOSAL SYSTEMS

LTD.

With exquisite slowness the hydraulic door begins to roll back over the top of the garbage truck.

Slurrpp! Forrest overcomes his paralysis and pulls one grimy leg out of the waste. He tries to turn and move sideways.

Above him the bale begins to slowly push out.

Goddamn! It's so close he can see the license plates!

Sloorrp!

And then comes a different sound. The hydraulic whine stops, the truck seems to shimmy and lurch! The motor revs higher! Blinking through his rain-splattered glasses he sees the four rear tires of the garbage truck spinning on the slick edge of the wall. The truck twists . . . .

Slurrrp, sloorp!

"Please . . . I'm sorry," says Forrest as the bale vibrates up and down and twists as the truck's engine revs into a screaming sound, the tires smoking, the huge truck shifting, sliding now *over the edge* of the wall, gathering speed as Forrest's face goes slack.

He is caught, stilled, silent as the monster vehicle begins to tumble down the wall.

Forrest stands, waiting beneath its gigantic shadow. Waiting, doomed, with one leg stuck up to the thigh in the waste—

"I'm sorry, kid," he says too late.

STEPHEN E. MILLER is an actor and writer living in North Vancouver, B.C. His written work has appeared in numerous periodicals, and his play *A State of Grace* was produced by Vancouver's Tamahnous Theatre in 1982. As an actor, he has had principal roles in a number of films, including *Cousins, Betrayed, The Accused, Iceman,* and *Immediate Family*. His stage work includes roles in *Romeo and Juliet, American Buffalo, White Boys, True West,* and *Of Mice and Men.*

Wastefall won the 12th annual Pulp Press International 3-Day Novel Contest, written during the 1989 Labour Day weekend. His work was interrupted by two dinner parties, but he still managed to finish ahead of the Monday midnight deadline, and had a "great time" doing it.

The **Pulp Press International 3-Day Novel Contest,** the world's most infamous literary marathon, takes place during the Labour Day weekend (the weekend of the first Monday in September) on typewriters and word processors all over the world.

The rules are simple: Entrants, having filled out a registration form and paid an entry fee of $7.00, begin writing at 12:01 a.m. Saturday, and must stop at or before 12 midnight Monday. The novels may be written in any location and using whatever method except handwritten, so long as it takes place during the three prescribed days. If you cannot type, or do not have access to one, you are permitted to get your handwritten novel typed during the week following the contest. Entrants then return their finished novels to Pulp Press sometime during the week following the contest, accompanied by a self-addressed stamped envelope and a statement signed by a witness confirming the novel's completion over the Labour Day weekend. The winner is announced October 31. First prize is publication and instant notoriety.

For registration forms and/or more information, send a self-addressed stamped envelope (or $1.00 if outside Canada, as non-Canadian stamps are not usable) to: